SERIOUSLY DEAD

Ghosts of Carrington
Book 2

Maddie James

Sand Dune Books

SERIOUSLY DEAD

Ghosts of Carrington, Book 2

Maddie James

Seriously Dead
Copyright © 2023, Maddie James

Editing, Formatting, and Cover Art by Jacobs Inc, LLC.

First Edition, May 2023

All rights reserved.

The unauthorized reproduction or distribution of this copyrighted work, in whole or part, in any form by any electronic, mechanical, or other means, is illegal and forbidden, without the written permission of the publisher. This is a work of fiction. Characters, settings, names, and occurrences are a product of the author's imagination and bear no resemblance to any actual person, living or dead, places or settings, and/or occurrences. Any incidences of resemblance are purely coincidental.

Published by Maddie James, Turquoise Morning, LLC, DBA Jacobs Ink, LLC.
P.O. Box 20, New Holland, Ohio

Maddie's VIP Insider News

Be the first to get the news about my books—new releases, free ebooks, sales and discounts, sneak peeks, and exclusive content! Just add your email address at this link:
https://maddiejamesbooks.com/pages/newsletter

Seriously Dead

Another deadly romantic comedy—three sisters, a smattering of ghost, a touch of romance, a boatload of mystery, and a stitch of southern humor.

Molly Campbell had everything—a gorgeous Louisiana mansion, a rich husband, and a lucrative career. Had—not has—because her redneck husband dies in a seven-car pileup on the way to a monster truck pull, setting off a chain of events that leaves her penniless and moving into her deceased Gran's home in Carrington, Louisiana.

To say lifestyle change is a bitch is an understatement.

She misses Don (and admittedly, his money) but doesn't miss his belittling manner.

When he comes to her in ghostly spirit and apologizes for every nasty thing he's ever done (too little, too late), and that he lied to her about the bank account (too little, too gone), and tells her she needs to pay off his casino debt to keep the family safe (too overwhelming, too damn much!), and suggests that the truck accident might not have been an accident after all (too creepy, too murdered?), she gives him the cold shoulder.

Molly has no desire to listen to her deceased husband's honeymoon phase sweet-talk and probable lies in death. She'd had enough of that while he was living.

But Don insists he was murdered, and when things start happening—eerie phone calls, threatening messages, and bullets whizzing past her on Gran's porch—Molly concedes.

With her sisters in tow, and aided by a charming, tattooed private investigator, Molly seeks to uncover the truth. The suspense and hilarity that ensues might make you laugh out loud—seriously. Dead serious.

Chapter One

"Geez, Molly, do you have to be such a damn needy drama queen?"

Molly Newberry Campbell swiped her nose on her sleeve and looked up at her sisters. She'd just finished a very ugly, hiccupping cry, and had laid her hot, damp cheek flat against the cool lacquered tabletop. The fact that she'd recently downed a little whiskey didn't help. Their corner of the bar was semi-dark, with a smoky haze haloing the lights above them. She squinted first at Marla, her oldest sister, then at Mitzi, the middle sister, and gave them a half-drunk serious stare.

"Actually, yes I do," she slurred. "I just buried my freakin' husband. I deserve needy."

"But we don't need drama queen."

"And it's been two months."

"Plus, you didn't like him much near the end."

"That's not true!" Molly sat up straight in protest, then slid back, planting her face square on the bar.

The youngest Newberry sister, Molly had been babied by the family to some extent—she knew it and didn't deny it. She'd always been coddled, and well, she liked playing the helpless act when she could get away with it. And when they weren't babying her, they generally chided her for her dramatics—but over the past few weeks they had taken super good care of her, and she had no clue how she would repay them.

Tonight, was one of those nights.

"*Only* two months," she reminded, talking into the bar top.

Mitzi sidled up to her. "She's right, Marla. Cut her some slack."

"We were supposed to get her mind off things tonight, not relive them," Marla reminded.

"I love y'all..." Molly drawled, raising up. She took another long sip of her Southern Comfort and ginger ale, fished the Maraschino cherry out with her forefinger, popped it in her mouth and flung the stem away to the floor. Blinking, she stared at her sisters through her brain fog. She wished things were different—but was secretly grateful for the closeness she and her sisters had recently rekindled.

That's what sisters did in a time of crisis. Right?

Even if they were blunt and a little mean girl to her occasionally.

Tragedy. It was all such a tragedy. Everyone said so.

Marla patted the back of her hand. "You know we're here for you, Molly." She shrugged and glanced at Mitzi. "We're always here for each other. Dysfunctional family, or not."

Dysfunctional? She supposed they were. Not every family could say they'd hid a dead body in their Gran's freezer with the blackberries or had witnessed a deceased ex-brother-in-law come back to life in front of their faces.

They were, indeed, unique. That was what one called dysfunctional southern families, right? Yes. They were unique. Sounded a little quirkier and a lot more acceptable put that way.

But as for always being there for each other?

"Well n-not always...." Molly stuttered. "There was that

time that y'all wouldn't bail me out of that blind date with Jimmy Henderson's cousin and I was literally *dying* to get out of the back seat of that old Chevy of Jimmy's at the drive-in over in Athens." She turned to Mitzi. "You remember, don't you Mitz? Gawd. Why do guys think that kissing after eating onion rings is an okay thing?"

"That's a night I'd rather not relive."

Molly hiccupped. "Me neither. Onion ring French kisses are not good."

Mitzi snorted. "That was the night you hooked up with Don, remember? Once we'd snatched you and whisked you away with us to the bowling alley?"

"But not soon enough." She sniffed. "Jimmy's cousin damn near popped my cherry that night."

Marla spit her swallow of beer on the bar table. "Shit. I didn't know it was that hot and heavy."

"Not on my end. Thank God you two got there in time. Saved my ass again." She paused, remembering that night and how awful it was at the drive-in. And later, after meeting Don, how the tables had turned. *He was so nice back then.* "Oh, Don..." The sniffling started again.

"Ah, shit, Mitzi," Marla said and elbowed her in her side. "You are an idiot."

Something stabbed Molly straight to the gut. She could do nothing but moan. *Oh, Don...* Mitzi rushed in closer. "I am so sorry Molly. I wasn't thinking. I shouldn't have mentioned him. I'm an insensitive bitch. I...."

"I can't believe he's gone!" Molly shrieked.

Turning heads registered in the periphery of her brain. She was likely about to make a spectacle of herself in one of Carrington, Louisiana's only home-grown pubs. But the locals would understand, wouldn't they? After all, everyone knew Don. Of course, they knew her, too. Or remembered her. She'd been the only double homecoming queen at Carrington High for decades. Both basketball and homecoming. People *knew* her. And *knew* Don. They *were popular*.

No. Prominent, as her mother would say. Popular was for teenagers. Prominent was for townsfolk.

"Oh, my stars! What am I going to do without him, girls? I mean, I have the kids, and the house, and the business and not to mention all those cars and his big-ass trucks and...."

She hiccupped and slugged back the rest of her whiskey. "I am doomed. My life is over. And my poor husband, mangled up in that seven-car pileup on the interstate. He didn't deserve that."

"Yeah," Marla said. "A semi load of watermelons can sure put a damper on things."

"Good God, Marla!" Mitzi put an arm around her little sister, turning to her. "I know honey. No matter what, Don didn't deserve to die like that. It's going to be tough. You're just lonely now and vulnerable. Things will get better. It's too soon to think that you could get over this so quickly. Give yourself—"

"I hate that bastard husband of mine!"

Marla and Mitzi both jumped back, eyes wide, and Molly almost giggled at their startled faces.

She straightened her back. She might have had one too many whiskeys, but she still enjoyed shocking her sisters. "Well, it's true. Sonofabitch had to go and die. Ripping my life right out from under me. Nasty, belittling, liar of a man. I am more than mad. I am livid!"

And then she broke down and sobbed. "Oh gawd. He's gone. The bastard is really dead. Seriously. Dead."

"Seriously," Marla repeated.

"Dead," said Mitzi.

Molly laid her hot cheek flat against the table. "Yes. And I'm seriously in a pack of trouble."

Out of the corner of her eye, Molly watched her sisters look at each other, shrug their shoulders, and lean into the table.

"Okay, I'll bite. What kind of trouble, Molly? Spill it," said Marla.

Molly glanced from one sister to another. "Oh, I can't. It's so damn embarrassing."

"Look." Marla leaned closer. "You know you're going to have to tell us eventually, because likely we'll be bailing you out, so just go on and say the words."

Molly sucked in a breath and attempted to sit up straighter. "All right."

"Well...?"

"It's money. I have money problems."

"But Don was loaded."

"Was, being the operative word, I guess. Dead guys aren't still loaded."

"But didn't the money go to you? He had insurance, right?" Mitzi peered into her eyes.

Molly shook her head. "Nada. Nothing. No. Apparently not. And it appears he was in debt up to his pretty blue eyeballs."

"Holy shit on a shingle."

"I guess he'd been gambling. There's this guy from the casino who keeps coming by the house to collect."

Marla cocked a brow. "I didn't know Don gambled."

Molly shrugged. "Me, either. Except that he and Tom—you know, his business partner—had been spending a lot of time at the casino lately. Don said it was business, but now I wonder. How many construction deals are made over a blackjack table, really?"

"This is not good, honey." Mitzi bit her lip.

"I know."

"Do you know the guy?"

Molly shook her head. "Never saw him before."

"What did he look like?" Marla edged closer.

Molly sighed. "Tall, bald, tattoo sleeves—looked like he lifted weights."

"Shit." Marla stood. "Okay, we're going to need to find out more information about this guy, who he works for, and exactly what he wants."

Time to fess up, Molly guessed. "Oh, I know what he wants."

Mitzi leaned in. "Spill it, sister."

"Fifty thousand dollars, the Grave Dodger, and to exhume Don's body."

Molly watched both her sisters' eyes grow big, round, and wide, while they jerked up into ramrod straight sitting positions.

"What? That's insane."

Molly agreed. "That's what I said. Can't get blood out of a turnip, as they say. Stiff bodies, either."

"I mean digging Don back up. Why?"

Molly shrugged. "Make sure he's dead?"

Marla sat back against her chair again. "Wow. He is dead. Right?"

"Deader than a doornail. I made sure of that. I pinched him twice in the casket to be sure."

"Good God, Molly."

"Well, I needed to know! He was such a liar. What if he was faking?"

Molly glanced from one sister to the other. Marla still looked shocked and worried about the whole thing. Mitzi seemed to be deep in thought, then she spoke.

"We have to figure out how to get the money to pay this guy off."

Marla drummed her fingers on the slick tabletop. "What about the construction business? What's happening there? Have you spoken with Tom Purdy? I guess you own half of the business now, right?"

"I have no clue. Tom won't return my calls."

Mitzi stood now. "In two months, he hasn't returned your calls?"

"No." Molly shook her head. "I figured he was busy."

"Oh, Jesus take the wheel," Marla exclaimed. "You need help... And this is getting a little weird."

"But you've talked with your attorney, right?" Mitzi stared.

Molly sat silent, watching her sisters' faces.

Marla scooted closer. "Look into my eyes, little sister. You have talked with Jackson Cooper, Don's attorney, right? You have started settling this estate. Correct?"

"Ummm."

"Oh, shit, Molly. What the hell?"

Molly threw up her hands. "I figured I had time!"

"Well, you don't. You need money. And you need to know where you stand with all these financial issues. I'm calling Jackson first thing in the morning and we're getting an appointment."

"No."

"No?"

Molly laid her hand over Marla's on the table. "No. Don't call Jackson. I don't trust him."

"Why?" Marla studied her face.

"Because..." She took a deep breath, then let it out slowly. "Because he cornered me at a party at his house last summer and made a very serious pass at me. Like, tongue in my mouth and hand sneaking up my dress kind of pass. It was gross, like Jimmy Henderson's cousin with the onion rings."

"What the hell?"

"What did you do?"

"Slapped the shit out of him and pushed him off me. He was

drunk, so it wasn't hard. He fell back into a cabinet with glass shelves and broke some expensive knick-knacks. His wife, Grace—you remember her, former Miss Mississippi right?—was furious and yes, we made a scene. Don, the bastard, laughed it off. The next week Jackson came to the house to pay me a visit while Don was at work and told me if I ever tried anything like that again, I'd end up in the lake."

"Swimming?" Mitzi questioned.

Marla slapped her shoulder. "Good God, no. Bottom of the lake is what she means—with cement block shoes, I imagine. Oh shit, Molly. We must get you out of this mess."

"You need some serious money."

"Or we need to catch these guys at—something."

Molly thought for a minute. "I still have my job. And I suppose I could sell my Cadillac if I had to...."

One of Mitzi's brows raised. "Seriously? Can you raise that much cash selling Marty Lyn cosmetics? Plus, you need the caddy for work, so don't sell it. But being a consultant will not sustain your lifestyle, will it? I mean, I know you do well peddling mascara, but will it keep you in wine and mani-pedis and private school for the kids?"

"And pay off your tattooed debt collector?"

"Or buy out Tom Purdy?"

"And keep Jackson Cooper at bay?"

Molly shook her head. "Unfortunately, no. The hard truth is the bank started foreclosure on the house last week. My checking account is nearly dry, and the credit cards were all cut off."

"You're broke."

"I'm broke." She took another gulp of her drink. "And worse, I had to ask Mom if I could move into Gran's house."

"Oh, God, you didn't. What did she say?"

"The usual. You know."

"We know," Marla and Mitzi echoed.

Molly closed her eyes and tipped back her head. As if the mess Don left her in wasn't bad enough, dealing with her mother's southern snark about nearly *everything-in-the-world* was a bit more than she could handle now. "I'm so screwed."

"Yep. Screwed like a pooch."

Chapter Two

A week later, Molly pulled her lavender Cadillac up to the curb in front of her Gran's house. Stepping out of the vehicle, she shut the driver's side door and straightened the jacket of her best Marty Lyn pink and lavender suit. Head held high, she rounded the rear of the vehicle, opened the passenger back door, and ushered her three children onto the sidewalk.

Each child did as they were told. They waited there, by the car—dressed to perfection, hair coifed and styled, clothing starched and pressed, shoes spit-shined and polished—for their mother to guide their next move.

Magnolia, the oldest at eight years old, wore a pink summer sundress with matching sandals. Her long brown hair was swept up in a top ponytail, adorned with a big-ass, sassy southern bow. The sandals and bow were also pink, of course, matching the sundress.

Macey, her middle child at age six, dressed similarly, except her sundress was yellow, and she sported two side ponytails with equally large yellow bows.

And Don, Jr.—who they sometimes called Junior—wore a

little man suit, gray like his father's, that looked a mite ridiculous on his three-year-old body. He'd find a mudhole soon and the suit would be history.

But first impressions were important, you know? And while this was not the first time she and her children had arrived in her Gran's neighborhood—this was the first time they were coming here to live. And God knew the gossip mill nonsense would run amok as soon as the moving van arrived with their boxes and a few pieces of furniture.

They might be stepping down a notch on the social ladder, but at least they were doing it in style.

Molly moved to the rear of the car and popped the trunk, but before she lifted their bags out, looked at her children's sad, confused faces.

Smiling, she said, "Chin up!" She motioned with the back of her hand under her own chin. "This will be a good day, children. There. Yes. That's a good girl, Magnolia." Her oldest was catching on quickly. She was going to have to keep an eye on that child. In a few years, she'd be chasing away the boys. Oh, but Don would deal with those boys.

Her heart sank. No. Don would not be here to deal with any boys. She was on her own.

With a deep sigh, Molly returned to the trunk. She lifted several pieces of luggage out and set them on the sidewalk. They were all lined up there, like Mama bear, and Baby Bear suitcases in descending order of height. Of course, there was no Papa Bear because Papa was....

Molly shook off the thought. She had to buck up and move on—for the sake of those three Baby Bear children standing on the sidewalk staring at her.

Slamming shut the trunk lid, she clicked the button on the key fob to lock the car.

Straightening her suit jacket again, she tossed back a head

full of curly auburn locks and tilted her chin up. With three quick movements, she flicked up the handles on each of the child-sized roller bags. Nodding to them, she said, "Grab your bags, children. Shoulders back. Follow me."

They proceeded toward the house, following the old brick sidewalk—Molly, then Magnolia, Macey, and Don, Jr.—heading for Gran's front porch. This was the neighborhood Molly had grown up in but left when she and Don married. Her parents lived two streets over. It was not the most upscale neighborhood in town. Those half-million-dollar (or more!) houses sat on the outer fringes of Carrington, where Don had built their house. But The Woods Estates, where Gran and her parents lived, was a great neighborhood. Stable people. Upper middle class. A mix of blue and white color workers.

The children would do well there, she knew. After all, she had fared well, being a product of this area of town.

But as she stepped forward, Molly knew she was eating a bit of crow. She'd snubbed more than one neighbor over the years and had alienated the rest with her uppity, rich bitch, socialite attitude. She would have to mend fences.

Somehow.

In her mind's eye, she pictured every one of her Gran's neighbors peeking out from behind draperies and crab apple trees and fences, doing their best Gladys Kravitz impersonations. She could hear their whispers.

"Molly Newberry is slumming, I see."

"Molly Newberry, back on Elm Street? What a lark."

"Poor thing, reduced to living at her Gran's. Tsk tsk. And with all those children."

"You know, I heard Don left her penniless."

"Bless her heart."

"Let's take her a pie."

She dared any of them to bring her a damn pie or bless her

heart. All they would really want was more scoop and hoping she would spill. No. Not happening. Not yet, at least. Still, in the back of her mind, she knew that if anyone reached out to give a damn or a pie—or worse, a casserole—she might find a friend.

Having a friend in this neighborhood might not be a bad thing.

Tipping her chin a little higher, Molly didn't look right or left or—gasp—backward. She looked forward, knowing that her children were following, rolling their little bags behind them. She led the way up the steps with the grace only a southern born-and-bred woman could pull off. Crossing the porch, she unlocked the door, silently wishing her Gran would greet her on the other side. She could use a smiling, friendly face right now, and a little bit of unconditional love.

But Gran was gone.

Don was gone.

And they were here.

***

Hours later, after the unpacking and an evening of homemade pizza and an old VHS movie of Gran's—*The Ghost and Mrs. Muir*, to be exact, through which the children mostly slept—Molly lay in her bed staring up at the ceiling.

No, not her bed. She hadn't moved her bed with her.

Her bed was a king-sized monster with four mahogany pillars for bedposts and a wrought-iron canopy. It was so damn big it took four men to set it up in her house and when they did, they knew that there was no moving it again.

Besides, moving it was up to the new owners, if that was what they chose to do. She'd sell it with the house, which was going on the market next week. Plus, she'd sold most of the furniture and the housewares and a good bit of her high-end, designer clothes over the past week, too, piecemealing items out to the highest bidder over social media.

A very public display of neediness, Mitzi had told her.

Marla said she'd been practical.

She needed cash, right?

All that was neither here nor there now. The bed—her and Don's bed—was out of her life.

Ironic.

Don had told her they could never, ever move again, because that bed wasn't going anywhere. He never wanted to sleep in any other bed again, anyway, for as long as he lived—which turned out to be an accurate statement. He never slept anywhere else—except for the occasional hotel stay during a truck pull competition.

Now he's sleeping six feet under.

Frowning, Molly swiped away a pesky tear.

So, the bed had stayed. Molly had grown to love it, too. It made her feel even smaller than she was. And with Don sleeping next to her, she felt safe wrapped up in his arms.

At least they'd always had that. They never went to sleep angry with each other. They just fought like hellcats during the day, whether they needed to, or not.

But today, there'd been no fighting and tonight, there would be no cuddling or lovemaking, and she couldn't sleep.

Damn bed. She felt gawky and vulnerable in Gran's full-size, antique cherry, dainty four-poster—complete with a twenty-five-year-old mattress and her great-grandmother's Amish Star quilt. Gran's bed. In her grandmother's bedroom. In her grandmother's house.

Her kids were down the hall, each in their own rooms. Exhausted when she put them to bed, she'd hoped they would crash-out for hours. She needed rest, peace, and quiet.

If she could only sleep.

Couldn't.

Wide awake.

"Dammit. Might as well get up."

She tossed back her covers and swung her legs out of the bed. Pulling on a bathrobe, she padded out of her room and down the upstairs hall, peeking into each of her children's bedrooms along the way. Junior had a room to himself, and the girls shared a bedroom.

Molly picked her way down the stairs, avoiding the steps that creaked—she'd remembered those from when she was a kid—and hurried into the kitchen. A low night-light was on at the counter, providing a path to the stove. A cup of chamomile tea might do the trick, if there was any tea at all left in the house.

Gran had been gone for a couple of years, but Molly's mother refused to sell the house (lucky for her!) or change anything in the house or do much with it except clean. For that, Molly was thankful. She pulled a box of mixed teas from the cupboard and located a chamomile bag.

"Good. Thank you, Gran," she whispered. "Or Mom." She knew Gran had always kept a plentiful supply and variety of teas, and her mother had followed suit. She also knew her mother escaped to the house occasionally—supposedly to clean—but enjoyed her own cup of tea and a quiet hour in Gran's kitchen or sunroom while she was there.

Dad was retired, now, and there were days she just needed to be alone—without her husband underfoot.

The tea brewed. Molly settled into Gran's old rocking chair in the living room, sipping from her dainty China teacup. The floorboards creaked a little as she rocked, while her mind rolled over her current situation. Truth was, she'd been in limbo ever since Don's fatal accident.

She'd had it all—an enviable marriage, a gorgeous, well-decorated, stately Louisiana home built by her very rich hubby's construction company, and a lucrative career selling Marty Lyn cosmetics. She'd lived a privileged life for the past fifteen years.

Lived.

That was the past, because her rich redneck husband went and got himself killed on his way to a truck pull competition in Athens, Alabama, where he'd gone to showcase his famous Grave Dodger pulling truck. The wreck, which started the chain of events that left her penniless, with three young children to raise, and moving into Gran's house, was a turning point in her life.

The once-luxurious mansion that had been her home was almost gone, soon on the market to pay off Don's debts—some of them, anyway. Tom Purdy still avoided her calls, and she knew she couldn't put off talking to him much longer. She also needed to settle Don's estate—and had to find a new attorney to guide her through that. Jackson Cooper was not her choice, and of course, she didn't want to work with him, anyway.

And here she was, spending her first night in Gran's old house, a small and cramped space that barely fit her and the children and their possessions—even though they had severely downsized.

No worries. They would survive.

Builds character, her mother had told her the day before. She was right, of course.

But—to say lifestyle change was a bitch was an understatement. At least she was still regional manager for Marty Lyn and owned her lavender Cadillac free and clear.

If she would admit it, though, even though she loved the man and he gave her so much, she was slightly glad to be rid of Don.

For a few weeks prior to his death, she'd grown weary of his nasty belittlings. In short, he'd been dangerously close to hitting on her last nerve.

Her eyes grew misty.

A soft rasp and a creak sounded behind her. Molly blinked and stopped rocking, frozen to the spot.

One of the kids?

Another creak. From the stairway?

Turning, she blinked again, and stared at a translucent form hovering in the doorway, barely visible in the dim light of the room.

"Molly, I need to talk to you." The voice echoed softly in the stillness.

Don? What the f—

Closing her eyes tight, Molly sucked in a breath. *Calm down. You're just conjuring up things. You just watched a ghost movie, right? This is not real.*

"Molly?"

That was definitely Don's voice.

She abruptly stood, not taking her eyes off the apparition. The seat of the rocker shot forward and hit the back of her calves. She stumbled to her left, nudging the accent table there with her hip. Her tea sloshed over the side of her cup and into the saucer, splashing onto her fingertips. She set down the teacup.

The apparition reached for her arm, as if to steady her. His grip dissipated as it hit her flesh. *What the...?* "Don?" Her voice cracked. She reached for the light.

"Don't turn on the light. You won't be able to see me."

"But you're dead. I pinched you and everything in the casket, to make sure."

"Yes, I know. That was a bit comical, to be honest. But damn, woman, do you not trust me so much that you had to have proof of my deadness?"

Molly sighed. "What do you want, Don?" Her tone was clipped.

"I need you to know something." He stepped closer. "I never wanted to hurt you. I know I wasn't always the best husband, but I loved you, Molly. I still do."

Molly rolled her eyes. *I can't believe this is happening....* "Save it, Don. You had plenty of chances to make things right when you were alive. Now it's too late."

"Honey, sweetheart...."

"Oh, don't you go honey sweethearting me, Don Campbell!"

"I just want you to know that I'm sorry for everything."

Molly crossed her arms and huffed. *Am I supposed to just melt at his apology?* Just because he comes to me in ghostly spirit and apologizes for every nasty thing he's ever belittled me about? *Too little, too late.* Plus the fact that he lied about the bank accounts and credit cards? *Too little, too gone.*

Turning, she gave him the cold shoulder. "Look, Don. I have no desire to listen to your honeymoon phase sweet-talk in death. I had enough of that while you were alive."

Don's expression darkened. "You don't understand. I was involved in some sketchy things—most of them not of my own making—but regrettably, I was involved. Things that could put you and the kids in harm's way."

Molly stood straighter, her interest piqued. "You bastard. What kind of things?"

Don hesitated, as if weighing his words. "Some rather dubious business deals, I'm sorry to say. How do you think we got so rich? I wasn't always the man you thought I was."

Molly felt her heart sink. She had suspected as much, but hearing it confirmed by Don's ghostly form was a shock.

"What do you want me to do about it?"

"Find out what happened to me, Molly. Clear my name

where you can and fess up for my wrongdoings where you can't—make sure our family is safe. I might not always have made the right choices, but my intentions were good. I always took care of my family."

She had to admit that he did do that. But Molly scoffed. "And how am I supposed to do that? I'm not a detective."

Don shrugged. "I don't know. But you're smart, and you're resourceful. You'll figure it out."

Molly sighed. She wasn't sure what to do next, but she knew one thing for certain—she couldn't let Don's death go unresolved. She owed it to him, and to their family, to find out the truth.

Plus, it was up to her now to keep herself—and her children—safe and cared for.

"Okay, Don. I'll do it. I'll find out what happened to you and do the other things."

Don's ghostly form began to fade. "Thank you, Molly," he whispered. "I knew I could count on you."

She stared after him into the empty hallway. She wasn't sure how she was going to solve Don's murder, but she knew one thing for certain—she wasn't going to give up until she found out the truth.

Glancing at the mantle clock over the fireplace, she decided it was too early to call her sisters. Tomorrow was another day.

Chapter Three

Soon after she dropped the children off at day care and summer camp the following morning, Molly sat on the top step of Gran's porch and sent a group text message to her sisters.

Molly: *9-1-1. Gran's house. Stat!*

Immediately, the three little dots under her words started jumping.

Mitzi: *WTF, Molly? U OK?*

Marla: *On my way.*

Mitzi: *Out the door already.*

Marla: *Do we need coffee?*

Molly: *Made some. Bring donuts.*

Mitzi: *Who the freak stops for donuts during a 9-1-1 emergency?*

Molly: *Just get over here. Stat!*

She figured Mitzi would get there first, because she lived the closest, only five minutes away. Marla would need a little more time since she lived across town.

Mitzi: *I'll stop at the Coffee Caper for pastries.*

Molly: *Good. This will be a high-carb discussion. Need fuel!*

Marla: *And caffeine. Do you have the high-test stuff?*
Molly: *Is there anything else?*

The dots stopped and her phone grew silent for a minute. No wait. Shit. Dad. He frequented the Coffee Caper most mornings.

Molly: *Dad alert. Avoid at all costs!*
Marla: *Good point. He will ask questions.*
Molly: *Don't tell him a thing!*
Marla: *Like Mitzi can keep her mouth shut.*
Mitzi: *We don't know anything!*

Her phone fell silent, and Molly darkened the screen and sat it next to her on the porch. Glancing about, she took in the neighborhood, the sun streaking through the trees, flowers gently wafting about on a soft breeze. It was a warm morning already and promised to grow even hotter as the day grew on.

Summer in the south. Humidity. Heat. Bugs.

Carrington had all the above.

Gotta love it. Nothing you can do about it. The price paid for living near Louisiana wetlands.

Molly inhaled and squeezed the button on her phone to flash the time. Three minutes since her initial text. She figured she had approximately three more minutes before Mitzi would arrive.

She studied her neighborhood a little closer. Mrs. Pierson's house sat catty-corner from Gran's on the corner of Elm and Hemlock. When they were younger, they always called her house the picket fence house, because of the white picket fence that surrounded her front yard. Over the years, the roses planted along the fence grew to the point they nearly covered the fence, and basically served as a horizontal trellis.

And there she was, Mrs. Pierson herself, pruners in hand and wearing her sundress and straw sunhat, moving from rose to rose, trimming and clipping and talking softly to them—in turn lifting her gaze to glance about and gather intel on the neighborhood.

Molly smiled and stood, then waved. She ambled down the porch stairs and took a few more steps along the sidewalk. When she was young, Molly thought Mrs. P. old back then. She figured she was probably in her late seventies now.

"Hello there, Mrs. P.," she shouted. Might as well get a head start on the impressions. Good or bad.

Mrs. Pierson lifted her head and shot her gaze at Molly. "Hello, dear. Nice morning. Isn't it? How's your grandfather?"

Deader than a doornail. Molly smiled. She'd always had a crush on Grandpa Joe. "Just fine, Mrs. P. You?"

Her neighbor's head shot up from the rose she'd been examining. "Got a touch of diverticulitis if you must know. Keeps me from shitting but then again, maybe that's better than the alternative." She returned her attention to the rose.

"I see." Shoving her hands deep into her shorts pockets, Molly took a few more steps toward the curb, halting beside the Cadillac. "Beautiful morning, though."

"Yes, indeedy." Mrs. P. nodded. "I hear the band will come by around noon. I love those trumpets."

Looney. Tunes. Molly smiled and glanced both up and down the street, watching for either of her sisters to appear.

A car slowly turned the corner at Elm and Hemlock and parked by the curb at Mrs. Pierson's. The vehicle looked slightly familiar, but Molly couldn't place it—and she couldn't see who was sitting in the driver's seat, either. The live oak in the yard shadowed the windshield, it's canopy rather large. Molly watched Mrs. P. lift her head and angle toward the car, too, giving it a stare.

Mitzi pulled up from the opposite direction, windows down, with country music blaring from the cab of her new Silverado pickup truck. She parked behind the caddy. Molly turned in her direction and momentarily forgot the mystery vehicle down the street.

She rushed down the sidewalk.

Mitzi rounded the front of her truck. "I brought provisions—plenty of sugar and carbs. Blueberry scones, chocolate eclairs with that thick cream filling that you love, glazed and powdered donuts, and some random pastries. Plus, three more extra-large coffees just in case we need them. Basically, I told Clara to throw one of everything in a bag or box. I didn't know if there was much coffee here, or if you'd been to the grocery yet, so I brought more." She jerked open the passenger side door. "Oh, and no Dad. He'd already left this morning. Dodged that bullet."

"Good God," Molly exclaimed, looking in at the passenger seat. "Look at it all."

"Well, we all know we don't cry 9-1-1 unless it's something serious, and I had no clue how long we would need to talk, so...."

True statement, that. "I'll grab a couple of bags and a box."

"I've got the coffee."

Both women stepped back from the truck with their arms full. Down the street, a motorcycle squealed around the corner, passing the mystery car, and parked in front of the caddy. Marla revved the Harley's engine twice before shutting it off.

Molly caught Mrs. Pierson's facial scowl from across the street. *Oh, well. There goes my reputation....*

Marla threw her leg over the back of the bike and stood, fiddling with the strap on her helmet. Removing that, she placed it on the back of the bike and faced her sisters. "Well?"

Mitzi tossed her head toward the truck. "Grab those last two boxes of pastries."

"Will do." She retrieved the boxes and nudged the truck door closed with a sharp swing of her hip.

"Thanks." Molly faced her sisters. "You two will not believe what happened last night."

Abruptly, a gunshot ripped through the otherwise calm morning, shattering a ceramic flowerpot on Gran's front porch. Mrs. Pierson's ungodly scream echoed down the street. Mitzi dropped the coffee cups, hot liquid splashing on the brick sidewalk.

"Shit!" Marla jumped back.

All three women spun as the mystery car maneuvered a screeching U-turn and sped away. All Molly got was a glimpse of taillights as the vehicle left.

"What the fuck?" Marla exclaimed.

"I just peed my pants," Mitzi said. "And squashed the scones."

"I think Mrs. P. fainted on her roses."

"Oh, my God. Is she shot?"

All three women stared for a frozen second, then dropped the pastries and ran.

* * *

An hour later, the sisters watched one of Carrington's finest police-officers-in-training exit the porch and head toward his official Carrington police cruiser parked behind Marla's Harley. He'd taken their statements, eaten their donuts, and drank the last of their coffee.

Mrs. Pierson was tucked into bed before the officer arrived. She was confused and disoriented after fainting into the roses, although a bit scratched, but none the worse for the wear. Marla, being the taller and stronger of the sisters, had carried her into her house and deposited her on the sofa, while Molly called her daughter, who lived around the corner on Maple Street. She thanked them profusely for taking care of her mother once she'd arrived, then shushed them away with a wave of her hands.

The three stood side-by-side on Gran's porch, arms crossed, following the cruiser's progression down the street as the officer drove away.

"This has been an interesting morning," Marla exclaimed.

Mitzi toed at some loose dirt on the porch floor. "That was the pot we got Gran for her birthday a few years ago."

"At least the fern can be repotted, I think," Marla said. "Of course, what do I know? I kill plants."

Molly signed. "Well, his digging around in the dirt for the bullet rather disturbed the old girl, I'm sure."

"The fern is a girl?" Mitzi turned to her sister.

Molly shrugged. "Well, duh, yeah. Fern? It's a girl's name, right?"

Rolling her eyes, Marla turned and headed inside. "Good grief, Molly. C'mon, let's get inside."

Mitzi nudged Molly and they followed their older sister into the house.

Once there, Molly locked the door behind her. "One can never be too safe," she murmured.

"Except your enemies can obviously shoot through things so...." Marla smirked.

"Just find a seat," Molly directed. "I've got more troubles than a mystery shooter."

"Which we need to talk about."

"Yes, but in a minute. I need to tell you the other thing first, and then maybe we can fit the pieces together."

Marla sat on the sofa and leaned back against the menagerie of throw pillows Gran had always kept there. "What's going on, sister?"

"And what could be worse than a shooter?" Mitzi sat beside Marla.

Molly intentionally chose an overstuffed side chair opposite them. After a minute of staring, she finally said, "I need to find out who killed Don."

Marla leaned up, her elbows perched on her knees. "Don was killed in a traffic accident, Molly. Key word here—accident."

She shook her head. "No. He was murdered."

Mitzi and Marla exchanged glances. Mitzi asked, "And how do you know this?"

"He told me."

"Before he died?" Marla squinted. "Like, he warned you that someone was out to kill him, or something?"

With a huff, Molly stood. "No. No, nothing like that. I had no clue he was in any kind of danger, fooling around with shady business deals—but it seems he was. I have theories about who may have done it, but nothing concrete. That's where you two come in."

Both sisters stood, talking at once.

"Oh no, not me."

"Count me out."

"Naw. No."

But Molly begged, moving closer. "Please? You must help me find out what was going on. Who killed Don and why, so he can rest in peace, and I can get closure. Plus, he said finding out the truth will keep me and the kids safe."

"He said?"

"Yes." Molly nodded. "He told me last night."

"Last night?" Mitzi's voice pitched higher.

Molly eyed them both. "Yes. Last night. He came to me."

Both sisters scowled.

"Like what, in a dream?"

"No." Molly shook her head. "I couldn't sleep, so I got up for tea."

"And...?"

"And Don came to me. I saw him. Not his full-on body and all, of course, but sort of an image of him standing in the doorway, but it was his voice."

"What the heck kind of tea were you drinking, my sister? Perhaps a bit of cannabis?"

Molly exhaled and waved Mitzi's question away. "No. Chamomile."

"You mean he was a ghost." Marla leaned forward. "Don came to you, to tell you something, as a ghost."

Nodding, Molly grasped both sisters' hands. "Oh God, yes. He was a ghost. And he needs my help."

Marla dropped Molly's hand and stepped backward, pacing off to the side. "Of course he does. He treated you like shit when he was alive and now that he's dead, he needs you? Oh, this is real peachy, Molly. You told him no. Right?"

Molly bit her lip and held Marla's gaze.

"Molly?"

"I told him I would figure it out."

Mitzi threw up her hands. "Molly, you can't figure your way out of a paper bag. How are you going to play detective and figure out who killed Don?"

She drew her lip further into her mouth.

"Stop doing that," Marla said. "You always did that when you were a kid, when you wanted something. That pouty, lip biting shit will not make a difference here, this time."

"My kids aren't safe. He says I'm not safe. And someone shot at us this morning."

"But they missed," Mitzi said.

Molly swung toward her. "But maybe next time they won't."

"That was a warning shot, I'm sure." Marla continued to pace. "Hells bells, Molly. I wouldn't even know where to start. Do you?"

It hit her then, suddenly, that she did. "Yes. I know where to start. Grab your things." Molly headed for the front door, snatching her keys off the hook by the wall and her purse from the entry table.

Mitzi jogged up beside her. "Where are we going?"

Molly turned at the door, one hand on the doorknob. "To the caddy. We're going for a ride."

* * *

Face it, Molly. You may have to come to terms with the fact that the man you married and thought you knew was not the man he seemed.

She stared ahead down the street, driving her lavender Cadillac toward downtown Carrington, a little lost in thought. The gunshot incident had frightened her more than she wanted to let on. In some ways, where they were going made her nervous, too. What if she found out things about Don she really didn't want to know?

But what if she found out things that explained what the heck was going on?

And what if what she found out things *she needed to know* to save her family?

She had to do it. No choice.

Reaching between Mitzi's knees, she downshifted the caddy as she turned the corner heading out of The Woods Estates, and onto the main road toward downtown. Both sisters sat up front, on the caddy's bench seat, their gazes pinned to the road ahead.

"Can you shift this thing a little smoother please?" Mitzi asked. "And stop touching my inner knees."

"Sorry." Molly glanced at her, patting the leather dash. "She needs some work. I don't have the funds right now."

Marla smoothed her hand over the deep lavender interior.

"The inside looks good as new. How long have you had this thing, Molly?"

She had to think back a bit. "I won it for top salesperson nationwide five years ago. I know, it's old, but it gets me around and I love it."

"The bench seat is a nice touch."

Molly smiled. "I had to special order that and pay extra."

"Standard shift, too?"

"Oh, yes." Molly nodded. "I enjoy shifting gears."

Mitzi glanced about. "Me too. Makes me feel badass. Except, this stick between my knees is rather uncomfortable."

Marla coughed. "Thought you were rather fond of sticks between your knees."

Mitzi swiped at her. "Not metal ones!"

"Well, I sure as hell hope not!"

"Ahem." Molly coughed. "Cut it out." She slowed the car and looked in her side mirror, flipped on her blinker, and prepared to change lanes. "Like I said, it was a special order. Not many bench seats with a retrofitted stick shift."

Her sisters glanced at each other.

"Hm." Marla looked out the passenger window. "A retrofitted stick might be interesting."

"Oh, stop it." Molly changed lanes and sped up.

After a minute, Mitzi piped up again. "Where is it that we are going exactly?"

"Juniper Hills."

Mitzi gave her a wide-eyed look. Molly could see it out of the corner of her eye. "You know I don't enjoy going there, right?"

"Too many memories?" Marla asked.

"Well, of course!" Mitzi crossed her arms and leaned her head against the seat. "My husband nearly died there, and it was hell trying to get him back to life. You remember. Right?"

"Of course, we remember. But it all turned out. Ken is alive and well now—no longer AWOL or a ghost."

Silence spread over the caddy.

"Shit," Molly spit out. "What if Don comes back from the dead too, like Ken did."

"Do you want him to?" Marla angled a glance around Mitzi.

Suddenly, Molly braked, realizing she was approaching a red light. She turned to her sisters. "No! I don't want him to come back to life. And that's the sad and awful truth!"

Marla and Mitzi stared.

"What? Am I a terrible person now? The man has anger issues."

Finally, Mitzi said. "Well, then. Bringing Don back to life will not be part of the plan. The light is green."

"Oh."

Molly drove and the other women stayed quiet for a few more minutes.

"You're lucky I'm on summer vacation, Molly, otherwise I couldn't do this, you know. I just can't leave the classroom on a whim."

"I know that. Thank you."

"And you're lucky Ken is out of town on business. You know how he gets testy when I'm away from the home office for too long.

"I know that too, and I thank you both very much."

Molly pulled off into an industrial area of Juniper Hills.

"Where the heck are you taking us?"

She didn't answer but drove further into an empty lot, rounded several long buildings with garage doors, and parked in front of storage unit number 1313.

"We're here." Molly huffed out a breath.

"A storage building?"

Molly nodded. "Yes. When I cleaned out Don's office at

home, I packed up everything in boxes and totes, and had them stored here. There has got to be information in all his stuff. Don't you think? Don had this unit for years. Let's go." She pushed her car door open and headed toward the unit and the padlock on the door.

The sisters spilled out of the caddy, too.

Cradling the lock in her left hand, she slipped the key from Don's key chain into the padlock.

"What do you expect to find here?"

Molly faced them. "I'm not sure, but it's a place to start. Tom Purdy has not returned my calls yet, so I can't get into his office at work."

"Put that on the to-do list, Mitzi," Marla said.

Mitzi nodded and made a check mark motion in the air. "Don's work office. Duly noted."

"You said he had this unit for a long time?"

Molly nodded. "Yes. Occasionally he'd pack up things at home and bring here."

"Did you ever come with him?"

Molly shook her head. "No."

"Do you suppose this is where he kept all his ill-gained money and other assets?" Mitzi grabbed both their arms. "What if there is a dead body in there?"

"Seriously?"

"I mean, you never know. You said Don had anger issues."

"But he was not a murderer." The thought of sleeping with a potential murderer was a bit more than Molly wanted to handle right now. "He was murdered. Remember?"

"Of course."

Molly pondered what might be inside, though, her fingers frozen on the lock and key. What if they found evidence that incriminated Don for something horrible? What if there was money stashed away inside? Could she keep it? Lord knows she could use a few extra dollars.

Mitzi squared herself in front of Molly. "Do you have any idea who might be at the bottom of all this?"

"No clue." Molly shook her head and turned back to the padlock, twisting the key in the notch. The padlock clicked, unlocking. Molly unhooked the lock from the door, stuffed it into her shorts pocket, then bent and grasped the door handle, flinging the thing upward.

The door rolled up with ease and rocked into position at the top of the unit.

The three sisters looked inside and gasped.

Chapter Four

"What the hell?"

"Excuse me. Is this the right unit?"

"Of course, it is. The key worked."

Marla stared at the key in Molly's hand. "Maybe it's a skeleton key and works on more than one unit. Molly, are you sure this unit is Don's?"

"Positive." Molly stepped inside the empty unit, turning in a circle, and looking in every corner of the room. "Thirteen was his lucky number. Double thirteen was especially lucky. He tried to use the pattern any time he could, especially when gambling or playing the lottery."

"Guess it wasn't so lucky the day he died. That was Friday the thirteenth, wasn't it?"

Molly ignored her. She didn't want to think about that day right now. Moving on into the unit, she slowly spanned the empty space. "This thing should be crammed full of Don's shit. At the very least, the stuff I had the movers relocate from his home office should be here. Where the frig is it all?"

Marla thrust out her hand. "Give me the key. I'm going to check the neighboring units."

With a sigh, Molly handed off the key to her sister, who without hesitation, headed outside toward the other units.

Mitzi caught Molly's gaze. "What is going on here?"

"I'm clueless."

"Wait." Mitzi rushed to the rear of the room and retrieved a manilla legal-sized envelope taped to the wall. "What's this?"

Molly moved closer. "It has my name on it."

"Damn straight it does." Mitzi pulled the taped envelope from the wall and handed it to Molly. "Here."

"It's sealed."

"Well, just rip it open."

Molly hesitated. "I don't know. Maybe we shouldn't touch it. Maybe there are fingerprints on it. Maybe there is awful news inside."

"And maybe there are answers."

Molly held the envelope with the tips of her fingers. "I think I have some driving gloves in the car."

Mitzi looked at her cross-eyed. "Why the heck do you have driving gloves in your car? We live in the south!"

"It's cold sometimes in the winter. Besides, frost."

"Which we rarely get." Mitzi gave her the standard eye roll and headed for the caddy. "Whatever. I'll get them."

Marla burst by her on her way back inside. "What's that?" She nodded toward the envelope.

"Did the key work anywhere else?"

Marla shook her head. "No. It's only for this unit, I assume. Looks like Don's stuff has vamoosed. Now, what are you holding?"

"But who in the world would take that stuff? It was only boxes of papers and odd random crap of Don's."

Marla shrugged.

Mitzi jogged back toward them. "Here are your gloves."

Molly held out her left hand while Mitzi put a glove on it.

Then she switched hands holding the envelope and did the same for her right hand.

"What the heck are you doing?" Marla asked.

"Trying not to disturb fingerprints."

"Oh, give me a break. Just open the damn thing."

But Molly had a sneaking suspicion she wasn't going to like what she found inside, so she wasn't in any kind of hurry. "Maybe I'll do it when we get home."

"Oh, good gravy, Molly."

"Would you just open it?"

Molly gritted her teeth. "Okay. Fine."

Handling the glued envelope flap with her leather driving gloves proved more difficult than expected, so she tore up more of the envelope than she'd wanted. But all the same, she got the thing open and looked inside.

"Well?" Marla paced a little.

"What's in there?" Mitzi strained her neck.

Molly looked inside, then tipped the envelope to empty its contents onto the floor. A key fell out and bounced on the concrete. Molly stooped to pick it up, then straightened and held it out. "A key."

"That's it?"

She nodded. "Yep."

Marla stepped closer. "Anything special about it?"

Molly shook her head. "Nope. Looks like a duplicate. Like one you would get at most hardware stores, or some such place."

"Maybe J.R.'s Hardware down the street. We should ask."

"I wonder if they keep records?"

Molly stared at Mitzi. "Seriously? How many people get duplicate keys made in a day? I'm sure there are no records."

"She's right." Marla approached and looked into Molly's eyes. "Put the key in the envelope and let's get back to Gran's. I have some thoughts rolling around in my head."

"Great."

Marla nodded. "We need to stop by the office supply store on the way back."

Molly dropped the key in the envelope and folded the thing over. "Why?"

"I need chart paper. Lots of it. Theories are swimming in my brain. Let's go."

The three headed toward the caddy.

"Oh goody," Mitzi said. "Are we going to make Venn diagrams and suspect boards and such?"

Marla halted. "Well, we're not going to diagram sentences."

"You *are* an English teacher."

Marla jerked the caddy passenger door. "Not today. Get in, sister." She motioned to Mitzi.

Molly reached for the handle on the storage unit door, pulled it down, and padlocked the empty unit. "Not sure why I'm bothering locking up," she muttered, then shrugged. "Oh. Well."

* * *

An hour later, Marla stood in the center of Gran's kitchen, staring at the various chart papers taped to the kitchen cabinets. Both Mitzi and Molly sat at the oak pedestal table sipping tea and eating scones. Watching Marla at work, when she was attempting to figure out stuff, was sort of mystifying.

She'd write something on a chart, then stand back and stare at it.

She'd glance at the other charts, right and left, then stare some more.

Then she'd pace, always looking at the floor.

After that, she'd gaze out a window, return to a chart paper, and add some new tidbit of information.

The sisters knew not to bother her when she was in this mode of operation—whatever mode it was called. After all, she was the one with college degrees (and frequently reminded them of that fact) so Molly and Mitzi simply went with it.

"So, here's the thing," Marla finally revealed. "Nothing clicks. Nothing connects. Everything is so...random."

"And it took you an hour to figure that out?"

Marla whirled to look at Mitzi. "I don't see you doing much."

"You told us to stay out of your way!"

Molly stood. "She's right. Walk away from the chart paper. Let's go over the facts as we know them—together—and then perhaps things will become clearer."

"Good idea." Marla parked her marker on the table. "Let me grab some tea."

They refilled their teacups and headed to Gran's frilly, semi-Victorian style living room—or the sitting room as Gran liked to call it—and found their respective chairs.

Marla liked Gramp's broken-down leather recliner, feet up.

Mitzi shoved fringed throw pillows aside and lounged on the camelback sofa.

Molly settled into the soft and comfy overstuffed armchair with doilies by the side table with the pseudo-Tiffany lamp.

"All right. Let's go over the facts," she said. "Verbally."

Marla huffed. "I really need to write things down."

"No. We're talking and brainstorming first, then things will come together."

Mitzi glanced at Marla. "When did she become the smart one?"

Shrugging, Marla returned, "Just go with it."

"Thank you," Molly said. She sure hoped she knew what she was doing. "I just need to talk this out, so listen. Please?"

"All right."

"I've probably left some things out. Previously, I mean."

"Well, sister." Marla leaned forward. "Spill it. We need to connect the dots."

Molly heaved a tremendous sigh. "So, I told you some of this, but not all. A few days after the funeral, I started getting eerie, breathy, hang-up calls from a restricted number. They always came to the house phone, not my cellphone."

"You didn't tell us that."

"No, because I didn't think it was important until now. Maybe it's something. I don't know. However...."

"Go on," Marla urged.

"Then the calls started coming from a bank in New Orleans —one that Don and I never used, or so I thought—about defaulting on the mortgage."

Mitzi squinted. "I thought you both banked here in Carrington, at Second National?"

Molly nodded. "We do. Did. I've nearly emptied our joint account, and I need to settle the estate before getting to the others."

"And the mortgage was closed there?"

"I thought we paid it off three years ago. Seems Don took out a second mortgage on the house—and then the mortgage was sold, apparently. I asked the bank how Don could have obtained the second mortgage without me signing, since my name is also on the deed, and Greg Abbot, our loan guy there, told me he didn't know. That he was not the person who handled that transaction."

"Don't you think that sounds fishy?"

"I certainly do." She shook her head. "I think maybe Don forged my signature or maybe completely left me out of it."

"Why would he do that?"

"I don't know." Molly stood, crossing her arms over her chest, and stared at Mitzi. "Obviously, he did not want me to know that he borrowed money against the house. I thought we owned it free and clear, but no...."

"And maybe the second mortgage thing is just a sham, someone trying to get money out of you, since the bank here in Carrington seems to be clueless."

"Perhaps. I hadn't considered that," Molly said.

Marla kicked down the recliner foot stool. "So, the money troubles go way back."

"Evidently."

"And Don has been making those payments."

"Until he wasn't."

"Then there is the casino debt."

"Oh, hells bells, that's right. I nearly had forgotten the tattooed debt collector who randomly showed up on your doorstep with demands."

"Yes. Fifty thousand dollars, the Grave Dodger, and to exhume Don's body."

"Wait." Mitzi scooted to the edge of the sofa. "Why would the casino want the Grave Dodger? It was messed up bad in the wreck, wasn't it?"

Molly nodded. "As far as I know. I've not seen it since they hauled it off."

Again, Mitzi scooted closer to the edge. "Hauled off where?"

"To the junkyard."

"Hal's Junkyard in South Carrington?"

"I'm assuming."

Marla caught Molly's gaze and held it. "You need to know these things!"

Mitzi jumped up. "If there is something in the Grave Dodger that Tattoo Man, or whomever he works for wants, we need to find it."

"Hold that thought," Marla told her. "There has to be more.

What about exhuming Don's body?" She looked at Molly. "Why would they want to do that? Did they do an autopsy?"

Molly shook her head. "Pretty sure not. They would need my permission for that. Right?"

"I think so." Marla shared a glance with Mitzi. "Maybe... Oh, I don't know but, maybe Don *was* murdered—poisoned or something—but whoever wants the body doesn't want others to find out, so if the body is exhumed they could steal it and get rid of the evidence."

"That's rather convoluted, isn't it? I mean, he's already six feet under."

"But if you go snooping around, and you decide forensics needs to be happen on the body, then it can be exhumed and tested for shit. I think. Hell, I don't know. I'd have to do some research."

Molly paced a little and waved her hands about. "No, no, no. We're going down a rabbit hole here. Put that thought on hold. Let's talk through the rest."

"There is more?"

Molly nodded. "Of course, there is more."

"Geez." Mitzi plopped back down on the sofa.

Marla deflated into the leather recliner. "Spill it."

"Okay. Tom Purdy."

"Don's business partner?" Mitzi eyeballed her.

"Yes. He won't return my calls. Hasn't since Don died. Strange, huh? I went by Two Dudes Construction a week ago and Jillie Dillon, their assistant—you remember her, right?—wouldn't let me in."

"Jillie Dilly? The most unlikely homecoming queen in forty years of Carrington High?"

"One and the same. But I digress. Anyway, she wouldn't let me in Don's office. Said it had been locked up tight ever since his death, and she'd been given strict orders from Tom—no one in or out."

"We need to get in there."

"If only we had a key."

Silence. The three exchanged glances.

"We have a key," Molly squeaked out.

"That we do."

"Another thing on the list." Marla cleared her throat. "Is there anything else you need to tell us, Molly?"

"Besides the fact that I haven't settled the estate yet? I suppose I should find out exactly what was in Don's will—in case there are some clues, or maybe answers, there."

"Not a bad idea."

"You both are going with me."

Marla released a huge exhale. "Okay. It's time to head to the chart papers again, but I'm going to sum up things for us first. Ready?"

"Yes."

"Go for it."

"All right," Marla began. "First, we need to go to New Orleans and talk with someone at the bank holding the new mortgage, if we can figure out what bank that is. Second, a trip to the junkyard is in order. Third, a visit to the local Medical Examiner to find out what happened with Don's body after the accident, forensics and such, if anything. Then fourth, to the casino to find out how far in debt Don was with them—or with someone who frequents the casino. And last, we need to see if that key unlocks Don's office."

"But maybe not in that order." Molly thought she should contact Jackson Cooper first, before all the other stuff. "I need to find out about the will."

"Right."

"And we need to figure out who took all the stuff from the storage unit, and why."

"True, that."

"In short, we have murder suspects," Mitzi said.

Molly blinked. "We do?"

"Sure. Tattoo Man. Tom Purdy. Jackson Cooper. Casino person. And any of their associates."

"What about the bank people?" This was all moving a little fast for Molly. How would she keep up with everything?

"I think they are simply collateral. Don needed money, which is why he gambled and ran up the debit, then he took out the second mortgage to pay off Tattoo Man."

"But he didn't pay him off, evidently."

"Right," Mitzi added. "So they axed him."

"And now they want his monster truck, or something in the truck, and Don's body." Molly had to think more about this.

Marla snapped her fingers. "Because there's something valuable there, somewhere. What? We have to figure that out."

"Wait." An idea popped into Molly's head. "Is the Grave Dodger worth money? I mean, in the condition it is in? Would just getting its carcass be what they are looking for?"

"You could be onto something. "Marla stared off toward the kitchen. "Even some money is better than nothing, and that is a pretty famous pulling truck—lots of awards and all and it was featured on that commercial—maybe selling it would get them some cash."

"Oh, hells bells. I have a headache." Molly rubbed her temples. "This may all be too much. I can't do this."

Mitzi moved closer, wrapping her arms around Molly's shoulders. "You're not alone, sweetie. We are in this together."

"I know."

Marla rubbed her chin, staring out the window again.

"Good discussion, ladies. We've landed on quite a list of suspects."

"How in the world are we going to figure this out?"

Marla faced them. "Only one thing left to do."

"What's that?"

"Hire a detective."

"Oh no, I can't afford that," Molly protested.

Marla shook her head. "No worries. I know a guy, and he owes me a favor."

"I hope it's a big one," Mitzi murmured.

Marla stared. "As a matter of fact, it is huge."

"Are we talking about the same thing?" Mitzi hiked a brow.

"Probably not." Marla waved her off and began scrolling through her phone. "Anyway, his name is Brody Willis. He's one of the best detectives in the area. Shall I call him?"

"Okay…" Molly nodded. "But wait. How do you know him?"

Marla met her gaze. "Oh, he's a regular at the bar I frequent in Shreveport."

"Great." Mitzi sighed. "Does he have tattoos and ride a Harley?"

Grinning, Marla winked. "Of course. Who else is my type?"

"Call him," Molly told her. He might be just the guy she needs, given the circumstances.

* * *

Well after midnight, Molly lay in the dainty four-poster bed and stared up at the light fixture in her Gran's former bedroom. The dim light from her bedside table cast an eerie pattern across the tiled ceiling. Random thoughts rolled through her head, like, did her grandparents have sex on that mattress, and would she ever have sex again?

She did like sex.

And she and Don had enjoyed a great sex life.

A *great* sex life. And sometimes, the more they fought, the better the sex. Sometimes, she wondered if he aggravated and annoyed her just so he'd get her riled and they could have wildly steamy makeup sex.

Did her grandparents have wildly steamy makeup sex on this mattress?

She squinted. Ewe. Not thinking about that.

"Penny for your thoughts, darlin'."

The voice floated over the bed. Molly sat up with a start. "What?"

Laughter followed. Don's laughter.

Molly scowled. "You son-of-a-bitch. You scared the shit out of me. Don't do that!"

A shadowy form settled at the foot of her bed. "You were thinking of our lovemaking."

Oh crap. He can read my mind?

"Sometimes."

"Shit, Don. This will not work. You can't be in this house reading my mind."

"Tell you what, sweetheart. When it comes time, I'll go away. But I'm sticking around until I know you've taken care of everything to keep you and the kids safe."

Molly sighed. "Well, it would help a whole hell of a lot if you would tell me exactly what happened, so I can actually take care of it."

The shadowy form drifted closer. So close, in fact, she wondered if that warm waft of air grazing her cheeks was his ghostly breath. She shivered and backed away a little.

"I would tell you if I knew. I don't. This is why I need your help, darlin'."

Hells bells. "What do you know?"

"This. I was heading down the highway, the monster truck on the trailer behind me, when things started going all cockeyed. I remember jerking the truck to the left, and feeling like I was going to black out. My throat closed and I couldn't breathe. My chest was tight. I remember sideswiping that semi and then everything went black. I don't know a thing that happened after that."

Molly studied him, or what she could see of him, anyway. Was that the image of his face manifesting itself in front of her?

"Don, one question. Why did you go alone? Usually, Tom goes with you. Why did he bail at the last minute?"

Ghostly Don fell silent for a few ticks of her bedside alarm clock. "He didn't bail. He was there."

"No. What?"

"He was there with me, in the passenger seat. At least that's how I remember it."

Molly shook her head. "No. Everyone said you were alone. The police. The medical examiner. Other people at the scene. No one mentioned Tom or anyone else with you."

"But he was there when we started out."

"I don't understand."

"Maybe I'm having difficulty remembering all the details, sweetheart, in my state of being here."

She figured dead was a good excuse for that. "It's okay, Don. I get it."

"Let me ask you this, sweetheart. Have you seen Tom lately?"

Molly swore she could see more of Don's features now. Something gripped her gut, deep inside. "No. I've tried calling. I even went by the office. He won't see me."

"Interesting."

Molly stared at the apparition, which was taking on a more solid form. "Don, I can sort of see your body."

"That's right. And as you get closer to figuring out the facts, you'll likely see me more clearly. At least I think that's how it may work."

Molly's brain spun. "So, Don? Is Tom Purdy involved in this? Is he the person I need to focus on?"

She could swear Don winked.

"You're getting closer," he said, then faded away.

"You bastard," Molly hissed under her breath.

"I heard that."

Molly plopped back to the bed and turned on her side, covering her head with the log cabin quilt.

Chapter Five

The next morning, Molly and her sisters stood outside Two Dudes Construction main office, located three blocks down from the storage units in the Juniper Hills Industrial Park, peering around the side of the old metal building.

Marla turned toward Molly, whispering. "So, you are saying Tom was actually in the truck with Don initially, and has been missing ever since the accident?"

"Or AWOL at the very least. Maybe lying low?" Molly shrugged. "Don wasn't super specific about that."

"It's a clue," Mitzi offered.

"For certain. Make a mental note," Marla told her.

"Sure thing." Mitzi stared off. "Clue. Tom Purdy."

"We have to be careful," Molly whispered. "We don't want to get caught."

"I really think we should wait for Brody," Marla said.

"But you said he couldn't meet with us until later tonight and I want to get a jump on things."

"Still, breaking into places is not our forte. Brody has skills."

"Not breaking in if we have a key, right?" Molly stared. "We just need to wait for Jillie Dilly to leave."

"I don't think that is an option. We may have to work around that."

"Look," Molly said, "I can't afford to get arrested with the kids and my job and all. It's an automatic withdrawal of my franchise contract with Marty Lyn if I go to jail. Some sort of contract item about adverse publicity. I can't remember. So, we have to be freaking sure we can pull this off and be doubly careful."

Mitzi rolled her eyes. "Oh, relax, Molly. It's not like we're breaking into Fort Knox. We're just trying to get some information about Don's death."

"Plus, you are, uh, were his wife. You have rights to his stuff."

"I suppose so but tell that to Jillie Dilly. Let's get this over with."

Marla nodded, a determined look on her face. "Exactly. And if the key doesn't work, then we'll find another way in."

Molly bit her lip, feeling anxious. "I just don't want to get in trouble. Don's death, and the hangup calls, and the flowerpot shooting, and the Tattoo Man showing up on my doorstep—well, it's all hard enough without adding legal troubles to the mix."

"You forgot the ghost of your husband showing up."

Molly thought about his appearance the previous night. "Yes. That too."

Mitzi patted her sister's arm. "Don't worry, Molly. We'll be in and out before you know it."

"All right. Let's do this thing."

They took a collective deep breath and crept around the corner to the front of the building, trying to look inconspicuous.

"Wait." Mitzi pulled out her cell phone.

"What are you doing?" Good grief, she'd just worked up her courage, and now they were stopping again?

"Hold on." Mitzi looked up at a sign on the side of the building and punched in the phone numbers there. Holding her phone to her ear, she waited.

A phone rang inside the metal building, the sound waffling through the open screen window above their heads.

"Two Dudes Construction, this is Jillie Dillon. How may I help you?"

Mitzi rushed back to the corner. The girls followed. Then she said, "Good morning, Ms. Dillon. This is Clara down at the zoning office. There seems to be an issue with one of your building permits. Could someone come down here and clear something up for us?"

"Oh, goodness," Jillie said. "One of my bosses is out of town though, and the other is...well, deceased. Is it something I can handle?"

"I'm pretty sure it is."

"Of course, then. I'll be right there."

"Thanks so much," Mitzi said into the phone. She clicked it off, and all three poked their heads around the corner. They watched as Jillie pushed open the heavy metal door to the building, swinging it wide open in a sweeping arc. She skipped down the steps and started across the parking lot.

Marla bent to pick up a large rock.

Molly gasped and whispered. "Don't kill her!"

"Are you an idiot?" Marla scowled and stealthily jogged toward the small porch, crouched beside it, and just as the heavy door was ready to close, stuck the rock between the door and frame. She glanced at the girls. "In case it locks automatically."

Molly exhaled. "Oh my God."

The receptionist spun out of the parking lot in her late model Honda.

"Go. Go!" Mitzi pushed at Molly.

The three women scrambled up the steps, opened the heavy door and pushed inside the building, glancing right and left.

Molly blinked, her eyes adjusting to the dim light, and pointed. "That way."

When they reached Don's office door, Molly inserted the key into the lock. "Come on, come on," she muttered, jiggling the key back and forth.

But the lock wouldn't budge. Frowning in frustration, she tried again, but still no luck.

Mitzi chewed her lip. "Maybe we have the wrong key."

Molly shook her head. "No, this is definitely the one we found in the storage unit."

With a look of determination on her face, Marla produced a small lock-picking kit from her back jeans pocket and got to work. Molly and Mitzi exchanged glances, then watched nervously as she inserted a slim metal tool into the lock and manipulated it.

"I didn't know you could do that." Molly stared, wide-eyed.

"I have many skills you don't know about, sister," Marla said, glancing over her shoulder.

Molly looked back at the front door. "I don't think I want to know."

A few tense moments passed, and then Marla grinned in triumph. "Got it!"

She pushed the door open and flipped on the overhead light, revealing a messy and cluttered office filled with files, paperwork, taped boxes, and plastic totes. The three sisters rushed inside, closing the door.

Molly locked it, just for good measure.

Mitzi raised an eyebrow. "Well, this explains a lot. Look at this mess."

"And now I know where the boxes from Don's home office went. I guess they delivered them to the wrong place."

"Or," Marla interjected, "they were intentionally intercepted and brought here so someone could go through them."

Molly snatched a stack of papers from the desk and stuffed them into her oversized purse. "Take all of it. It's evidence, and we don't know what is important. We may have to come back for the boxes later."

"Do you still have that key?" Mitzi called out. "The desk is locked."

"Ah." Molly bet that's what the key was for. "Coming."

And she was right. The key slid into the lock with ease and opened without effort. All five drawers of Don's desk were now open. "Get this stuff first," Molly said. "Lord, I hope we can carry it all. I don't want to make two trips."

"We can't. No time," Marla warned.

For the next few minutes, they stuffed files and loose papers into their overly large handbags.

"I can't get any more."

"This is enough to get us started," Molly said.

"We should probably lock up and leave for now," Mitzi said. "Once Jillie finds out that no one from zoning called, she'll be right back here."

Agreeing, Molly added, "Fine with me." She locked the desk again.

A loud rap sounded on the door, followed by a woman's voice. "Excuse me, is anyone in there? I was told to let no one in or out of this office."

Frick! Marla mouthed the word. *Jillie Dilly!*

The door handle jiggled loudly.

Mitzi's eyes widened in panic. "Hide."

The sisters scrambled, looking for a place. Finally, all three ducked into the wide kneehole of Don's overly large desk, holding their breath as the door swung open.

"Hello? Who is in here?"

A few silent seconds ticked by. High heels clicked on the floor, stopping to the left of the desk. The sisters stared at each other.

"Must have been my imagination," the receptionist muttered. More heel clicks, then a pause. "What is this light doing on?" She flicked it off, then closed and latched the door behind her.

Molly, Mitzi, and Marla let out a collective sigh of relief. Mitzi burst out quiet-laughing at their narrow escape.

"Shh!"

"Let's get out of here," Molly said, grabbing her purse. "I don't think my nerves can handle any more excitement."

They unfolded themselves and rose from under the desk, glancing about.

"Not sure how we are going to get by Jillie now," Mitzi said.

"Not an issue." Molly looked intently toward the rear of Don's office. "Looks like Don had an exit strategy. A back door."

The other two sisters rotated and stared at the door. They headed toward it.

"Grab a box or tote if you can," Molly said. "Quietly!"

They each did. Molly purposely left the door unlocked as they left. "Just in case," she told the girls. "Maybe we should come back later tonight for more."

"Good plan," they agreed.

As they stepped out into the bright sunlight, Molly felt grateful to have them by her side.

* * *

Later that evening, Molly sat at a table for four at Luigi's, looking down at the menu which boasted of *the finest Italian fare in all of Carrington*—which truthfully wasn't saying much for this small town of less than twelve-thousand people, and being that Luigi's was the only Italian restaurant in town—wondering when the rest of her party would arrive.

She glanced up, drumming her fingers on the white, starched tablecloth.

Her phone buzzed beside her plate. Swiping and entering her passcode, she glanced at the face. Text message. Then another.

She clicked to open the sisters' message thread.

Marla: *Sorry, I can't make it.*

Mitzi: *Me either. Ken wants to zoom tonight. He's out of town and it's sexy night tonight.*

Marla: *Geez. You plan sex?*

Mitzi: *We do when he travels!*

Molly: *I hate you both.*

Marla: *It will be fine. Brody is a nice guy. Very smart.*

Molly: *I bet. All the smart guys ride Harleys and have tattoos.*

Marla: *He has degrees!*

Marla: *And don't knock it sister until you've tried it.*

Molly rolled her eyes, then typed: *I'm more of the redneck country boy type.*

Marla: *[grinning emoji] Things change. Talk to you in the morning.*

Molly started to type a reply then didn't. Her phone fell silent. Seemed she was on her own tonight with Mr. Brody Willis, P.I.—who was late.

She ordered a glass of wine, then perused the menu one last time.

Salad? No. Lettuce sticks in her teeth.

Pasta? No. Carbs and calories.

Soup? No. No. Drippy and messy.

"Molly Campbell, I presume?"

Slowly, she angled her gaze low and to her right, noticing the fancy black-toed cowboy boots pushing out from under starched and pressed boot-cut jeans. She lifted her gaze up and up some more. The man, whom she guessed to be a few years older than her, wore a black t-shirt, form-fitting (and a nice form), topped off with a sharp lightweight leather biker jacket. His devilishly handsome look was made swoon-worthily complete with a scruffy-but-sexy five o'clock shadow, dimple in his chin, deep-set pair of ocean blue eyes, clean cut hairstyle, and a stupidly sexy grin.

All that and more tickled her fancy a little. Maybe a lot.

She wasn't exactly sure what she had expected—or maybe yes, she did, such as lots of leather, tattoo sleeves, maybe a chain or two, ponytail, and a skull cap, perhaps? But the picture of perfection standing before her totally conflicted with the image Marla had placed in her head.

"Molly?" the guy said again.

"Um?" She half stood. "Oh, yes. Mr. Willis?" She put out her hand.

He shook it and let go quickly. "Call me Brody. Good to meet you."

Molly sighed and sat. "Likewise. I think."

Brody Willis sat across from her and grinned. "What's good here?" He picked up the menu. "My first time."

"I haven't been here in ages, but the chicken parmigiana used to be very good."

He slapped his menu closed. "Good. That's what I'll have. You?"

She might as well. "Yes. I was considering that."

"Good to get that out of the way." He leaned closer. "Now, I understand you have some issues regarding the death of your husband. Tell me about it."

Molly nodded. "Okay."

"And I mean tell me everything you know."

"Of course." She stared into his eyes, and he mimicked her stare. "It may take a while."

He didn't flinch. "I have all night."

"Oh." Gracious, his sultry gaze lit a fire in her gut. Not good. Was Marla dating this Adonis, or was she just playing with him? Marla didn't generally attach herself to a man for any length of time. She was more of a catch-and-release kind of girl.

"Wine, sir? The lady already ordered a glass." Molly glanced up as the server set her glass of Merlot on the table.

"I'll have a bourbon. Neat," Brody said. Then he flashed another smile her way. "You were saying."

"Oh, sure. Yes. You want the details."

"I do."

Inhaling deep, Molly eased the breath out as she spoke. "It started the night I got the call from the state police about Don's accident...." She paused. He hadn't flinched a muscle, intent on her words.

"Go on," he said.

"Well, we thought it was an accident at first, but now I don't think so."

"Because?"

Geez. How much does she tell him? About ghostly Don, too? She wasn't sure about revealing that yet. "Well, some things have happened that make me wonder if there might have been foul play."

Brody Willis leaned closer, both his elbows on the table, encouraging her to continue with his intense gaze.

"You see, someone shot at us—my sisters and me. Then there is the thing about the money and the mortgage and the casino and the Tattoo Man. Top that off with my husband's business partner coming up missing, we think. No one has seen him in weeks. And my lawyer is an ass, so I haven't settled the estate yet. Don's office is full of stuff I *thought* I had moved to the storage unit, which was empty when I checked, except for a key which worked on Don's desk. We figured that out after we broke into his office, my sisters and I, and we stole, er, retrieved a bunch of files before we barely escaped his receptionist. That happened just this afternoon, of course, so I haven't looked at them yet. And then there were the hangup calls and not to mention the ghost in my Gran's house, which—" *Shit.* She hadn't meant to go there.

Brody sat back and whistled. "Man. That was a mouthful. I think you may need to start over again, and from the beginning. Let's break this out in chunks."

Molly sighed. "Okay."

"You mentioned files. I'll want to review them."

She nodded. "Of course. Whenever you like."

The waiter brought the bourbon. Brody ordered the chicken parm for them both. Molly didn't care, really, she was simply ready for things to move on. While there was nothing about Brody Willis that made her uneasy, talking about everything they needed to discuss in public, however, made her somewhat nervous.

"Maybe you should ask me some questions?"

He stared. "All right."

For the next twenty minutes, Molly fielded questions from Brody best as she could. Mostly they had nothing to do with what was going on, but she wasn't going to question his process. Their chicken parmigiana came, drinks refilled, and they continued the discussion while eating.

Molly had to admit she rather enjoyed their conversation, which at some point had turned away from her troubles with

Don, to regular banter between a man and a woman—like, where are you from, what do you like to do in your spare time, do you have kids, and so forth....

She did notice, however, that the conversation was a little one-sided. Brody wanted to know a lot about her personally, and she feared she may have given away a little too much information. While on the other hand, he hadn't opened up much about himself, even when asked. His responses were generally flip, clichéd answers, or avoidance all together.

The server came and cleared their plates, asked if they cared for dessert, to which they both replied they did not. Brody gave the man his credit card.

"Oh. I'm picking this up," Molly told him.

"You are not," he said.

"But I am the one considering hiring you."

"And you are my potential client. I'm picking up the tab. No argument."

Molly bristled a little. She liked to be viewed as an independent woman. She also enjoyed being treated like a lady. Don had always paid the bill, no matter what—he liked playing the bigshot—even if it felt rather chauvinistic. To be honest, she had no clue what was normal in this type of business situation.

Never mind, just let the guy be the man and pay the bill. Don't push it, Molly.

After all, you're nearly penniless....

The waiter brought the check, Brody signed, and he met her gaze, holding it for a couple of heartbeats. "Shall we go back to your place? I'd love to review those files."

Molly gasped a little, and then gave him what she hoped was a pouty, innocent grin. Chauvinism, be damned. "Why Mr. Willis," she began, with her best southern belle voice, "I do think my files may need examining."

***

It only took twenty minutes to drive from Luigi's to Gran's house. She drove her lavender caddy, of course, and he followed her on the Harley. Thank goodness she'd had the kids spend the night with her parents—she didn't have to worry about working late with Brody, going over the files and all, of course.

She wanted answers and hoped Brody would study the paperwork scattered on the dining room and kitchen tables and find some clues—or at least make some sense of the situation.

She left the caddy and waited for him on the sidewalk. He roared into the neighborhood, and she saw several lights go out in houses across the street. Easier to spy with the lights out, she assumed. Plus, no one can see you in the window.

Well. Let them stare.

Brody joined her, that steamy grin on his face again, and she hooked her arm in his as they made their way up the sidewalk and onto the porch. He waited patiently while she unlocked the door, and they went inside.

Immediately, and without a backward glance, he headed into the dining room, which was visible from the entry, and started flipping through the files and papers there.

"See anything?" She edged closer.

"Not yet."

"Want something to drink?"

He glanced up. "Maybe caffeine. Could be a long night. Got coffee?"

Nodding, she said that she did. "Coming up."

After a few minutes, the coffee made, Molly moved back into the dining room with two steaming cups. She set one beside him on a coaster on the table—Gran never let hot dishes touch her cherry dining table, and she wouldn't either.

Brody slowly turned to her, his gaze capturing hers.

Those damn blue eyes....

"There is evidence here of some sort of mortgage transfer. Do you have any other paperwork?"

"Maybe, in all this mess. Apparently, the mortgage was sold to a bank in New Orleans, I was told. The Louisiana Republic, I believe." Her gaze fell to his lips.

"I was afraid of that."

"Why?"

"Because there is no legit bank in New Orleans called the Louisiana Republic. I think this may be a scam."

"How do you know that?"

"I don't for certain, but there are a lot of banking schemes going around right now, with made up bank names, and I've never heard of that bank."

That caused a modicum of panic to swell up inside Molly's abdomen. "What paperwork do you need?"

"Anything with signatures," he said, squaring himself more fully in front of her, and taking a step closer. "Or perhaps anything notarized."

"Oh." Molly licked her lips, which were suddenly parched. "I took some legal-looking papers upstairs and put them in the safe."

"I see." Brody dipped his head a little.

"Um," she whispered, "In my bedroom."

With a forefinger, Brody tipped her head up. He angled closer, staring into her eyes. "Should we get them?"

"Uh-huh?" She barely nodded. *Molly, what are you doing?*

His mouth descended, lightly grazing her lips.

Molly eased out a tender sigh....

A voice boomed out from behind her. "Oh, give me a freaking break, Molly! This guy? What the hell?"

Don! She jumped back. "Whoa."

Brody dropped his hand. "Wow. Sorry. I guess I misread the signals."

"I was sending signals?"

"Well, yes. Like you haven't had much male attention lately and…."

"And that I was dying to be kissed? Touched? Made love to? Ravaged? How dare you!" But that was exactly the truth. He'd nailed it exactly. Had she seemed that desperate?

Did he want to nail her?

"Damn, Molly. Sorry. Like I said, I obviously misread the situation."

"Darlin'," Don directed to her. "He's not the guy for you. Just get this case solved and hopefully I'll come back, and we can be together again. I can ravage you. You know I can."

She looked behind her. There he was, on the other side of the table, all swirly and smoky and everything. Smirking at her.

"No."

Brody touched her shoulder. "No? And what are you looking at?"

She twisted back. "Do you not hear him?"

"Who?"

Don laughed. "He can't hear me, sweetheart. Only you."

Molly stared at Brody. "Never mind. Not what I thought. It's been a long day and I think the Merlot went to my head." She put a hand on his forearm. "Do you mind if we call it a night?"

"I can come back—that is, if you still want to hire me."

"Oh no, she doesn't, buster." Don interjected. "You don't need him, darling. Let him go his merry way. He's not what you need. I'm what you need. Remember?"

"Yes. I do." She directed that to Brody, ignoring Don. "Whatever your going rate is, I'll pay it. Double if we can get this resolved quickly."

"Great."

"Not fucking great."

Molly jerked a hopefully nasty stare at her dead former husband.

Brody moved to the entry and picked up his helmet from the hall table, where he'd parked it earlier.

"I'm sorry," Brody said. "I should have been more perceptive. It's not been that long since your husband's death, and I'm sure you are a little vulnerable because of it."

"Now, isn't he just a peach?" Don called out. "Don't fall for it, Molly."

She bit her lip and took a few steps toward Brody. "Look, I'm a mess, to be honest. But let's pick this back up again tomorrow if you are available. The files, I mean."

He grinned that steamy grin again. "I wish I could, but I can't. I have another case I'm trying to wrap up over the next few days, so I can then concentrate on yours."

"So, you want to tackle my case?"

He leaned in and said softly. "Honey, I'd love to tackle anything you want me to tackle."

She knew he wasn't talking about the case. "Brody, I'm intrigued by your innuendo, but honestly, I'm not up for anything more than resolving my husband's murder right now. I hope you understand. Down the road, maybe, once we've settled some issues and...?" *And I need to talk to Marla to make sure she's not interested in you.*

Brody grinned and winked. Leaning in, he lightly kissed the side of her cheek and whispered. "I understand, sweetheart. Business first, pleasure later. I'm a patient man."

He pulled back and Molly found herself, once again, lost in his blue-eyed gaze. "Yes. Great." Good Lord, the man had her tongue-tied.

"See you, say, next Monday?"

She nodded, speechless.

Brody let himself out the door.

Molly watched him amble down the sidewalk from the sidelight.

"What a dick. That guy wanted inside you."

Molly whirled. "You don't get to interfere in my life anymore, Don! Especially my love life. Go away!"

The house suddenly trembled and shifted a little, and a vase that used to sit on Gran's bookshelf unexpectedly sailed across the room and shattered into a million tiny pieces against the living room wall.

"Stop that!" Molly yelled.

Don's ghostly form swept over the dining table, swirling around on a dark gray cloud of willowy matter, and headed her way. It halted in front of her face.

Hands on hips, Molly stood her ground. "You don't scare me, Don Campbell. You never did in real life, and you won't scare me dead. Now, cut it out. I mean it."

The gray cloud withered and a bodily form semi-manifested in front of her. "You don't need a private investigator. You can do this on your own, Molly."

"Then you have to give me more information."

"All right. Find Tom Purdy. You'll get your answers there."

"But what about the casino and the money you owed to someone? And why in the hell did you take out a second mortgage with a fake bank without my knowledge? Did you plagiarize my signature? And is the Grave Dodger worth any money in the state it is in? Because if it is, I'm selling it."

The gray cloud dissipated.

Coward.

Suddenly, it hit her. Perhaps the casino business was related to the fake bank scheme? She just needed to figure out how Tom Purdy fit into all of this.

"If only you would quit sprinkling clues. Can you just tell me what's going on?"

Silence. No rumbling. No smoky apparitions. Nothing.

Molly clenched her fists and stomped her feet. "Argh! You drive me crazy!"

The house quaked again. A second vase fell from the shelf and broke into a puddle of porcelain shards on the hardwood floorboards.

"Stop it! That one was antique."

"Just letting you know I'm still around, darling."

"I hate you!"

"No, you don't."

I do. I truly do. The last thing she needed currently was a ghost with anger issues hanging around while she attempted to recapture normalcy in her life.

She glanced at the shattered vase.

The ghost-man needed counseling. For sure. Yes, counseling.

It was the one thing she'd nagged him about for years and he had, of course, refused. (Real men don't go to therapy.)

But dead or not, Don needed help controlling his anger.

Perhaps she should take the upper hand and see that he got the support he needed, deceased or not—because seriously, a ghost living in her house with control issues was not a good thing. She had to think about the children, too.

Right?

But where does one look for therapy for a ghost? Not the yellow pages, she was certain. Psychics? Paranormal experts? Ghost busters?

Gah. Impossible.

Bottom line, if Don Campbell thought he could bully his way into having sex with her again, he had another think coming.

No way she was having sex with a horny, angry, ghost of a dead husband, no matter how untouched and neglected she felt. Not when there was a very alive, and obviously handsome, sexy biker dude private dick poking around, eager to get into her panties.

What's a girl to do?

But the facts remain—

1) Don was a horny bastard who still wanted sex, with her, even in death. And she? Well, was it even possible?

2) If he wanted sex with her, then he *had to* quit being so damn evasive and interfering and help her solve his supposed murder.

3) Plus, therapy.

End of story.

After that, she might think about the sex part—if she could get past the dead part.

Chapter Six

Where the hell did all the money go?

Don's construction business was lucrative. He'd worked hard over the years to build it with his childhood friend, Tom Purdy. For years, they'd operated side-by-side without incident—they liked each other that much—and had landed some very large housing contracts together. Molly's family had enjoyed living off that income for many years.

She'd always thought of Don as a simple country boy who worked hard and played harder, even though he wasn't. He was more complicated than that. By the time they'd met—she was eighteen and he was twenty-one—he had polished that down-home personality to a T. But while he enjoyed pulling off that country boy persona—the beer drinking, truck racing, gun toting redneck—he had grown up quite the opposite.

His family had money.

Both his parents were killed in a small plane crash when he was twelve. His only living relative was his mother's brother, who lived outside Baton Rouge, and who took him in after the accident. Don was raised by a man who hunted, fished, farmed, and drank a lot of beer. He was carefree and unencumbered and Don's teen years were pretty much the same.

Rumor had it his parents left him money, but Don never pursued it. His uncle didn't think it amounted to much. His parents had been rich, he'd told Don, but they were also up to their eyeballs in debt, and when the estate was settled, there was little left. Once the construction business took off, Don said he didn't need it. That he'd make his own way in the world.

And he did.

Until he didn't.

As Molly sat at Gran's dining room table, surrounded by file folders and boxes of papers and old mail, she tried to make sense of it all. She'd pored over files and financials the past couple of days, trying to find any evidence of shady dealings. She'd work through the weekend, too, getting things organized for Brody—easier for them both to make some sense of this mess.

Sighing, she looked up from her work and gazed out the window. *Brody. Wow.* He had some sort of intense magnetic power over her, that was for sure. Despite the warnings from Don, she was looking forward to seeing him again.

Obviously, that wouldn't be until Monday. He was working on the other case, like he'd said. Marla and Mitzi were also AWOL. Marla had two days of mandatory teacher training in Shreveport. Mitzi ran off to where Ken was working in Texas yesterday and planned to stay the weekend. Molly figured they needed sexy time that didn't involve a computer.

It was Friday, so that gave her two more days of work over the weekend—on her own—to get her theories rounded up and her ducks in a row. There'd be no day camp for the kids, so she'd have to work around them.

Drumming her fingers on the cherry tabletop, she thought for a second, then picked up her phone and scrolled. After a minute, her mother answered.

"Hi, Mom."

"Molly? How are things going at Grans?"

She sighed. "Oh, fine. Trying to get my ducks in a row." She shuffled some papers on the table.

"Ducks?"

"Yeah. Financially. I think I need to find another part-time job."

"Oh, honey. You know we will help if you need anything. I'm so sorry you are going through this."

"I know, thanks, Mom. I am trying to get a resume together so I'm working on that this weekend. And by the way, letting me live in Gran's house is plenty helpful, so you've already done enough."

"Well, what about the kids? Are they adjusting?"

Molly shrugged. How do you know with kids? "I think so. I'm trying to keep things normal as possible. They are at summer camp and day care, but today is the last day. School starts in a week."

There was a pause on the other end, then, "Hold on, Molly. I'll be right back."

She waited, thinking she could hear mumbling in the background.

"Molly, dear?"

"Yes?"

"How about if Dad picks up the kids this afternoon and we keep them for the weekend? We were thinking of going to the lake. Okay?"

"Oh, Mom. They would love that. Should I bring by clothes?"

"Don't they keep swimsuits and other things at the lake house?"

"They do!"

"Then we'll be fine."

Molly glanced at the clock. "Tell Dad to pick them up at three-thirty. He knows the routine."

"Yes, we do. Honey, you have a good weekend and don't work too hard on that resume."

"Thanks, Mom."

Resume. Right. No chance of working hard on that. What would she put in a resume, anyway? Stay-at-home Mom? Make-up salesgirl? Amateur detective? She supposed she could talk up the high sales associate award.

Her thoughts trailed off. Not thinking about that now. She had more pressing matters.

* * *

A couple of hours later, Molly stood staring down at the table. Stacks of papers here, folders there, bank statements and more in the tote on the floor. She'd created some semblance of order—maybe, anyway, so they could figure out this mess. Who knew for sure?

Would she ever be able to find any substantial evidence of illegal business dealings?

Don's bank records were a mess, and the statements from the Second National in Carrington revealed few clues. There were the payments for the regular things—utilities, taxes, insurance, groceries, and the like—but as she dug deeper, she noticed two things. One, a consistent cash *withdrawal* of two-thousand dollars every month, and two, a *deposit* monthly of five thousand dollars from Louisiana Republic.

Interesting.

What was Louisiana Republic anyway, if it wasn't a bank, like Brody said? And why was the mysterious entity paying Don that much money? If they were a scam, they wouldn't be paying anyone. Right?

And where did that two-thousand dollars go every month? Wired to offshore accounts? Payments to criminals for God-knows-what? Was it gambling debt? Or just running money? Good Lord, he surely could have gotten by on a lot less than two thousand a week for gas and lunch and other trivial stuff.

But according to the bank statements, both the withdrawals and the payments stopped four months ago—two months before Don died. Had he refused to fork over money as he'd done in the past, and that was his demise? Was someone holding something over his head—blackmail, perhaps? And they withheld the deposits?

Too many unanswered questions. Maybe she would never know.

Molly looked away from the papers and stared out the window again.

"Dig deeper, Molly," she said out loud. "There have to be clues here, somewhere."

She continued to work tirelessly, pouring over documents, making calls, and following leads. Disguising her voice and using a fake name, she phoned the bank (they knew nothing about Louisiana Republic), contacted old acquaintances (they also knew not where Tom Purdy was), and local businesses Don frequented (seemed he always paid his bills), and did everything she could to uncover more evidence.

Just when she was about to give up for the night, a plastic tote slid from across the room, like it had been shoved by someone, and stopped beside her chair. No one was there, of course, but the movement frightened her so much that she literally jumped onto the seat of the ladder-back dining chair. Finally catching her breath, she glanced into the open tote to look at the files stacked inside.

A sudden gust of wind fluttered the papers and shoved some aside.

The partially exposed cover of one file caught her eye. The words Louisiana Republic were typed on the tab. Again, the papers shuffled, catching her attention.

Molly glanced at the window, and realized it was closed.

She looked up. "Don? Is that you? Are you trying to tell me something?"

Silence met her ears, but the urge to grab up the Louisiana Republic file was strong. So, she climbed down from the chair and retrieved the folder.

Opening it, she rifled through the paperwork inside—but nothing inside referred to the (fake) bank or the mortgage. There was a land contract, a couple of old deeds, a written agreement between Brody and a man named Hank Carola, and some other odds and ends of papers with notarized seals and filing dates.

Hm. Some of the filing dates were recent, within the past month.

What is all this?

Her eyes crossed just reading the tiny, legal-jargon print. Plus, she was too tired today to make any sense of it. Tomorrow. She'd be better rested then, her brain clearer.

"When the heck are some pieces of this puzzle going to fall into place?"

The plastic tote nudged her chair again.

"Don? What do you know? Talk to me, please?"

She waited, but he wasn't talking. She wondered why he was silent. Was he fading away? Was his job here nearly done? Was she finally getting on the right track?

Who knew?

She still had questions. Lots of questions. And with not much tangible to go on—except the Louisiana Republic file—she had to wonder if she would find anything more.

"Maybe I should go back to Don's office and look through those other boxes." She glanced at the clock on the dining room wall. It was nearly four o'clock in the afternoon. She wondered if anyone had noticed that the back door to Don's office was unlocked yet. While she truly didn't want to check during the light of day, the thought of sneaking around alone, in that area of town at night, held even less appeal.

It was a dangerous game, and right now she wasn't sure who to trust. Carrington was a fickle town with distrustful people. Many people had loved Don but only tolerated her.

Some didn't believe she could have attained Marty Lyn high sales associate of the year when she won the caddy. Rumors rolled around town that she'd made up the story and special-ordered the lavender Cadillac herself—or that Don had bought it for her.

That hurt. Gutted her. Her hard work was just that—her work. Don had nothing to do with it. But very few people took her seriously.

Perhaps she could use that fact to her advantage. No one expected her to be smart.

"What if this web of deceit extends beyond Carrington? And beyond Don, and is bigger than it looks?"

She needed Brody, that was for sure, and her sisters, who always made her feel like she wasn't alone. But none of them were here tonight. She *was* smart and capable, so she could do this. Right?

If there were other players involved, some of whom likely operated in Carrington, she had to be careful. She could be heading into dangerous territory.

But she also knew she wouldn't give up until she found the truth.

Focusing her attention back on the tote, she spotted another legal-sized folder with the words "Last Will and Testament" scrawled across the front.

"Now, where did you come from?" she whispered. She swore that file wasn't in the tote earlier.

She snatched it up, sucking in a breath and holding it, then opened the file. Don's will and related paperwork were inside.

Maybe this was it, the thing she'd been looking for.

Taped to the left side of the file folder was the business card of Jackson Cooper, Attorney at Law.

Grabbing her cell phone, Molly bit the bullet and punched in his numbers. Jackson Cooper was not her favorite person, but she'd put this off long enough, and she could put him in his place again, if needed.

"Cooper and Associates. Grace, speaking."

She recognized the voice of Grace Cooper immediately. Jackson's wife worked as his paralegal assistant. "Hi Grace. It's Molly Campbell," she said. "I need to speak with Jackson right away, if possible."

Slight pause, then Grace replied, "Of course. Hold please."

Molly listened to some sort of gawd-awful elevator music while she waited. In her mind, she quickly relived the scene at the party where Jackson had tried to kiss her, and subsequent chaos ensued. Grace was not the happy camper then, and likely was still not.

The phone crackled in her ear. Jackson spoke. "Molly Campbell, as I live and breathe. Well, well."

"I'll cut to the chase, Jackson. I need to speak with you regarding Don's estate. Soon."

She waited. Was that a small chuckle he emitted from the other end of the line? *Jerk.*

"Of course, Molly. Turns out the rest of my afternoon is suddenly clear. In fact, I've been expecting your call, sweetheart."

Don't sweetheart me, bastard. Molly bit her lip. There was a lot she wanted to say but didn't. "I'll be there in fifteen minutes."

* * *

Molly contemplated showering and dressing in her finest business attire, waltzing into the law firm's office with rings on her fingers and bells on her toes, as they say.

Then thought better of it.

Perhaps she should arrive looking like the penniless, near homeless person she obviously was. Impressions were everything, of course.

Just ask her mother.

Besides, she didn't want to do anything perceived as her coming on to him. It was going to be all she could do to keep herself from slapping the shit out of his face again, should he come any closer than her personal bubble—which she may have to define rather quickly.

Maybe Grace would stay in the room.

Who was she kidding? Of course, Grace would stay in the room!

So, jeans, t-shirt, sandals, and a ponytail were her attire. No Marty Lyn makeup or her signature pink and lavender suit. Luckily, she'd showered the night before, so she didn't stink—although she sort of wished she did. One way to keep the idiot at bay.

Her modus operandi was simple. Get information about the will. Find out what steps were needed to settle the estate. And get the hell out of Dodge before he tried to kiss her again.

Jackson's office was in an older Victorian style home near downtown Carrington. She navigated the steep steps to his porch, crossed the wide veranda, then twisted the antique doorknob on the heavy oak front door. Entering the office was like stepping back in time. The décor was dark, with wood-paneled walls, heavy brocade draperies, walls lined with legal books and periodicals, and low lamps that gave off very little light.

A receptionist lifted her head at her entry.

Grace Cooper stood behind her desk, to the left.

"Molly. So nice to see you again." Grace shot her with a saccharine smile and held Molly's gaze while plucking up a legal pad and a large file folder. "This way. Jackson is expecting you." She waved her hand toward the hallway and motioned Molly to follow her. "Or, I should say, we're both expecting you."

Nailed it! She figured Grace wouldn't let Jackson out of her sight.

Once in Jackson's office, Grace handed her the folder with the stamped and signed copy of Don's will. Both women sat—Grace to the left of her husband and Molly in front of his desk.

Jackson tilted back his chair, threaded his fingers together across his ample belly, and stared across the desk at her.

"I'll be brief," Molly said.

Jackson nodded. "It's a simple will, nothing too complicated. It covers properties, assets, bank accounts, and the like. All properties come to you. You can see a list of them on page two."

"Properties? More than the house?"

"Yes. Take a look."

She flipped the page, her finger following along to where the properties were listed. There were several addresses, two near Baton Rouge. She looked up. "Don owned these?"

"Yes." He nodded. "They were transferred upon death to you. All we need to do is the paperwork to get the deeds in your name."

Molly swallowed. Deeds? Would this have anything to do with the old deeds she found in the Louisiana Republic file? Maybe she wasn't in as bad a financial situation as she thought?

"What about his business? How is that handled with Tom?"

"Good question. He was in here yesterday, and...."

"Wait." Molly put up a hand. "Wait. Tom was here yesterday?"

Jackson hiked his chair up straight and he leaned over the desk. "Yes. Is that an issue?"

"It sure is. According to his receptionist, he's been missing for a few weeks. Hasn't been to the office since before Don's accident. I've tried repeatedly to get in touch with him and he will not answer or return calls." *And Don says that he... Never mind. Not going there.* "What did he want?"

Jackson stared. "He wants to buy out your half of the construction business."

"For how much."

"Six figures."

"How much exactly?"

"That's up for negotiation."

Molly froze. She didn't trust Jackson. No way would she let him handle this. She drummed her fingers on the wooden chair arms, thinking. "So, Jackson, is the business technically mine to sell? Don's half, I mean."

He nodded. "Yes, with a bit of legal juggling and some paperwork, it's yours."

"I see."

"What shall I tell Tom?"

She stared at Jackson. "Nothing. Don't do anything. If Tom wants to talk, tell him to come to me. I'll want an appraisal. I know you were Don's attorney, but you're not mine. If there is any negotiation done, it will happen through me, or my designee." She looked at Grace, whose pencil was flying across the legal pad. "Make sure you note that, Grace."

She looked up and met Molly's stare. "Got it."

Molly figured she might as well dive in for one more question. "What about his bank accounts?"

Jackson stared. "What accounts are you aware of?"

She didn't like him turning the questions around like this. "He had a business account, a personal account, and a joint account with me. All here at Carrington, Second National. That last one has been pretty much emptied. I need to check on the others."

"Depending on how they were set up, you may or may not have access."

"I'll find that out."

"Is that all?" Jackson leaned back again.

"Are there other accounts that you know of? *Louisiana Republic*, perhaps?

"No, but if you find out that there are, please contact me."

"So what are my next steps?"

"Find out about the bank accounts. If your name is not on the accounts, they may have to go through probate—there are ways to determine that we can discuss—then I can handle that for you, or you can get your own attorney. Same with the deeds. Up to you."

"All right. I guess that's it?"

Jackson hesitated. "No. It's not."

"We've talked about the property, his business, the bank accounts—what else could there be?"

Jackson glanced at his wife. Grace nodded back.

"What?"

"It's the trust fund—the one Don's parents left him."

Molly was puzzled. "What trust fund?"

"You don't know about the trust fund?"

She shook her head. "I have no idea what you are talking about, Jackson. Spill it."

He cleared his throat. "Molly, Don's parents established a

trust fund for him when he was very young. His uncle was the trustee, now deceased, and passed away about three months ago. Apparently, he contacted Don before he died, confessing that he'd been withholding the truth since Don was a kid, and that he'd been pulling from the trust for years to make ends meet.

He and Don reconciled, it seems. Don accessed the funds and completed the required paperwork for that trust to be turned over to you and the children upon his death, split four ways. You are now the trustee for the children's accounts. It's all detailed on page four."

Molly stared at Jackson, leaning forward. "How much?"

"Four million dollars."

"Excuse me?"

"Four million, Molly. A million dollars for each of you. It's yours."

She collapsed backward on her chair. "What the hell?"

Jackson edged closer, over the desk. "And if I were you, I wouldn't broadcast that fact. Don had a lot of friends, but he also had enemies. I know we are not friends, Molly, and sincerely, I regret what happened last summer, but I don't want you to get hurt. Lie low. Keep quiet. Watch your back."

The grandfather clock behind Jackson tolled the five o'clock hour. He stood. Grace did, as well.

"Wait. I have more questions."

He slipped into his jacket. "I'm not sure I can answer them, but go ahead."

"What was his uncle's name?"

Jackson sighed and flipped through the file on his desk, then looked up to Grace. "Do you remember?"

She nodded. "Hank Carola, I believe. From Baton Rouge area."

Molly sat back in her seat. Interesting. "And what bank? Would it be Louisiana Republic, by any stretch?"

He nodded to Grace again.

"No," Grace replied. "Louisiana Republic is not a bank."

Molly straightened. "That's right. It's not." She enjoyed acting smart.

Grace looked directly at Molly. "Louisiana Republic is the name of the trust. The trust is held at the Red River Bank in Baton Rouge."

Molly blinked, taking in what Grace had just said. "But..."

But if that was the case, how could the mortgage on the house have been sold to Louisiana Republic?

Wait. Had Don paid off the second mortgage with money from the trust account before he signed everything over to her? Maybe he borrowed the money against the house, was getting heat from Tattoo Man, paid off the casino debt, and then the second mortgage with the trust funds.

Maybe that was it.

As soon as she was home, she was having a talk with the ghost husband of hers.

But then...why was Tattoo Man still coming after her?

Unless....

Unless he wasn't from the casino. Maybe he was sent by someone else, and the casino story was made up? Intended to throw her off track? Scare her?

Shit.

She watched Jackson guide his wife toward the rear of the room.

"I'm sorry. Our day is done, Molly. Read everything over. I'll not make a move without your direction. But don't linger long on all of this. We've already lost a few weeks. You might not trust me, but there are others out there waiting in the wings you should trust even less. Be careful."

He motioned to his wife and then exited the office. What was it with back door getaway exits around here? Molly sat in the quiet, semi-dark office, dumbfounded, and relaxed against the hardback chair, staring at the rows of books behind Jackson's desk.

To her rear, she could hear Jackson's receptionist's fingernails clicking on her keyboard, ticking off the seconds.

"Well, I'll be," she whispered. "What the fuck just happened here?"

Chapter Seven

Molly intentionally took her time driving home, letting her mind settle around what she'd just learned—and pondered what should happen next. She needed her sisters right now. Damn them. They'd both abandoned her. How could they?

But as she braked in front of Gran's house, glancing at the dashboard clock, her hopes escalated.

It was after five o'clock and Marla should be home from her in-service day. One sister was better than none, any day of the week.

Snatching up her phone, she dialed Marla, hoping to reach her before she headed out for a night on the town—probably heading to her favorite bar in Shreveport. It was Friday night, after all.

Marla's phone rang twice before she answered. "Molly?"

"Hey! Marla. What are you up to this evening?"

"Oh, you know. The usual."

Molly hesitated, biting her lower lip. "I found out some things today."

"Like...?"

"Interesting, rather incredible, life-changing things."

"Seriously?"

"Yeah." Molly blew out a breath. "I met with Jackson Cooper. He had information regarding Don's will and what was left to me and the kids, and I learned some puzzling things about Louisiana Republic."

"The bank in New Orleans?"

"Not a bank. It's a trust fund. And it's not in New Orleans."

"What? I don't understand."

"Can you come over?"

Marla hesitated on the other end, not immediately responding. Molly knew she was likely infringing on Marla's social life. Finally, she said, "How about dinner? Let's meet at Henry's BBQ. Say, about seven?"

While Molly wasn't sure she wanted a crowd around while discussing Don's will, and the stuff she'd learned this afternoon, an evening out sounded rather delicious. "Tell you what, Marla. I'm definitely up for an evening away from Gran's dining room table."

"Excellent."

"I'll meet you at Henry's at seven."

"Wear something cute."

"Why?"

Marla laughed. "Just don't come as you are. Spiff yourself up a little, okay? Pretend you're the old rich bitch Molly."

For the first time in a while, Molly laughed too. "Sure. Later."

Marla giggled as she cut off the phone conversation.

* * *

Stepping out of the shower a while later, Molly towel dried and ran a comb through her hair. Sighing, she faced herself in the mirror, acknowledging she'd let herself go some the past couple of months. But that's understandable. Right?

Her curly hair needed a trim, and her eyebrows were overgrown—dangerously close to sporting a unibrow. Staring down at her feet, she also concluded she was long overdue for a pedicure. And while she couldn't do anything about her hair or the pedicure before meeting Marla, she absolutely was not leaving the house until those brows were under control.

That mission accomplished within minutes, Molly finished drying her hair, applied her makeup, and headed into the bedroom to find the right clothes for the BBQ place. Shorts? Not tonight. She'd worn shorts a lot lately. Jeans? Too hot. The yellow sundress? While super cute, she decided no—she'd have to wear sandals and her toes were not sandal-worthy right now. Finally, she settled on a pair of wide-legged pants, slip-on canvas shoes, and sweet little halter top that nicely showed off her tanned shoulders.

Stepping back up to the mirror, she studied herself. Not too shabby for a thirty-something mom and widow, she guessed.

"Lookin' good darling, but don't you think that top is a little skimpy?"

Molly whirled toward the voice. She saw nothing. "Where are you? If you're going to talk to me, you need to come out and play fair. Got it?"

"Now, that may not be possible."

She glared. "Make it possible, Don. I have some things to say and questions for you, and I want to look you in the damn eye."

Silence.

Despite her misgivings about Don, Molly still had feelings for the guy, even if she was grappling with the ethical implications of having a relationship with a ghost. She had always loved sparring with him because she knew it would eventually lead to blissful makeup sex.

Maybe she'd goad him some more.

But what of her attraction to Brody?

What about her loyalty to her husband? (*But he's dead, Molly!*)

Love triangle in the making?

No! That would certainly complicate things to gigantic proportions.

"Hot date?"

Molly turned her back on the voice and looked into the mirror. "No. I'm meeting Marla for BBQ ."

"Henry's?"

"Yes."

Don heaved a ghostly sigh. "I used to love that place."

With his sigh, Molly's hair lifted and tickled her shoulders. Was he that close? She turned. "Don. Back up."

Things started getting all swirly in front of her. The shape of his body came and went.

"Molly, sweetheart, do you have any news? Have you found my killer?"

"No, but I found out some interesting things today. Why didn't you tell me about the trust fund, the properties, and all the details of your will? Would have been nice to know before I put the house on the market, sold most of our furniture, and uprooted the kids!"

Don didn't immediately respond. "I suppose you are right. Thing was, darlin', I hadn't planned on dying, so I didn't see the urgent need to tell you."

"Ha! More than likely, Don Campbell, you didn't want to tell me in case you needed to dip into that healthy trust fund your parents left you to pay off some debt you ran up."

"Well, I already did that, sugar. I paid off the gambling debt."

"So Tattoo Man wasn't from the casino?"

"Tattoo Man?"

"Some guy who came to my house wanting fifty thousand dollars, the Grave Dodger, and to exhume your body. What's up with that, Don? Huh?"

"Oh. Shit."

Suddenly, Molly could see Don a little more clearly. "I can see you."

"Maybe because we're getting closer to the truth."

"Is that how it works?"

"I'm not sure, Molly. Let me try something." He paused, and she watched his image. "I'm going to confess to you all that I know."

"That would be a breath of fresh air."

"My uncle Hank kept the trust from me until about six months ago. I knew very little about it until then. There was talk, but Hank said it didn't amount to much of anything. He lied, then felt guilty because he knew he was dying—cancer—so he transferred everything left to me."

"Go on." She already knew most of that.

"So, I kept out a lump sum in cash and paid off the casino. I'll admit, Molly, I was way over my head and the consequences for not paying would not be pretty. I had to get that taken care of, so I used that money. The rest I put in the account in your name only, and the three trusts for the kids, which you control. I figured if we ever needed anything more, I could borrow from you."

"Because you knew if you created a joint account, you couldn't keep your hands off it."

"That's right. And I hoped knowing that I couldn't easily

access that sizeable sum of money would keep me away from the poker table."

Suddenly, Molly realized she could see Don. His body was barely translucent, and he was almost human-looking. "Don? Is that really you?"

"You can see me?"

He drifted closer, looking nearly as handsome and as young as the day she met him over twelve years earlier. Immediately, she was drawn to him, like she'd been back then. "Yes. Confession must be good for you."

"Good for the soul, perhaps. Or so they say. Maybe mine is a little less black now."

He stroked the side of her cheek with his forefinger and surprisingly, she wasn't repulsed by the ghost-man's sweet gesture. "I have one more thing to confess, darling. Well, two."

"Okay?"

Don leaned in, brushing his lips across hers, and the sensual tingle that radiated from her lips to her gut, to the very tippy toes of her feet, consumed her.

No. No. No.

"Stop, Don. I can't. No."

He pulled back and his nearly formed body remained. "I understand, darling. It is a lot to grasp, isn't it? As much as I would love to strip you naked and take you to bed right now, I know it's not for the best. Look. The money is in the Grave Dodger. Get it. It's yours. Get the house back if you can. Take care of the kids."

More money? "What do you mean, Don?"

"Go find the Grave Dodger, sweetheart, get the money—and possibly, my murderer. It's time for me to go."

"Wait! You said two things."

His image shimmied in and out, and his voice came to her a

tad weaker. "Embezzlement, darling. Find Tom. Pay him. Then your problems will be solved."

Then poof! He had vanished.

Sonofabitch!

And for some crazy reason, Molly knew that Don Campbell was truly gone from her life. A wave of sadness fell over her she wasn't sure she could shake.

* * *

The moment she saw Marla sitting at the table in the restaurant, Molly felt relieved. Rushing toward her, she sat beside her sister on the picnic table bench and leaned in for a hug. "Oh my goodness, I am so happy to see you!"

"Good gracious, Molly," Marla exclaimed, nudging her away. "Are you okay? You know I don't do hugs."

"I know. But I needed a hug, so I was hoping you would reciprocate."

Marla stared at her, then leaned in and wrapped her arms around her. "You okay?" she whispered after a minute.

"No. Yes. I mean, I'm fine now."

"So, tell me what's going on?"

"Don is gone. I think he left Gran's house, and I guess is going off to do whatever ghosts do in the afterlife. I know I won't see or hear from him again."

Marla stared. "Is this good or bad?"

Giving her sister a half shrug, Molly said, "I think it's a little of both. I'm sad but also realize it's probably best he moves on."

"For him or for you?"

Molly thought about that. "For both of us."

"Wow. Did he have any last words?"

"He did. He said—"

A shadow crossed their picnic table. "Excuse me, ladies. This bench taken?"

Molly's gaze slid across the table to the tall, dark, and tattooed man standing on the other side. *Brody Willis.* He might be slightly rough around the edges, and older than her she'd bet, but he seemed ethical as heck with a kind heart. She supposed a girl could do worse.

If a girl was looking. She wasn't.

"Brody?"

He locked in on Molly. "Mind if I sit?"

"Oh, of course." She glanced at Marla, who shrugged. "Did you call him?"

Marla hesitated. "I, uh... Well, yes. I will confess. I gave him a call."

"Oh." Molly glanced between the two of them. "Oh! So you two are on a date."

Immediately, Brody shook his head and Marla elbowed her sister. "Not a date," both Marla and Brody echoed at once.

Marla continued, "We're just good friends, Molly. No dating going on here."

Eyeing her sister, she nodded, then said, "I see. I think."

Brody reached his hand across the table and touched hers. The sparks that landed on her fingertips were almost palpable. "Marla told me you had news. I thought I'd join you if that's okay."

She pulled back her hand. Sparks were distracting, and she needed to focus. "Of course. But I thought you were busy until Monday."

"Things are wrapping up on the other case. I'm good to spend some time with the two of you tonight. Besides, a guy has to eat, right?"

"I suppose that is true."

Brody held her gaze, and that simple act almost made her giddy inside. Then Marla interrupted.

"Well, I have an engagement later at Cooter's, so let's order and get on with it."

Molly gave her sister the eye. Engagement or hook-up? Hm.

Brody signaled the server who took their orders and left, then Marla jump-started the conversation.

"Molly, tell us what you know."

"All right." She shared about her meeting with Jackson Cooper, the truth about the Louisiana Republic trust fund and the money left to her and the kids (she purposely didn't tell them how much, in case there were other ears listening), and finally about how Don confessed he'd used some of the trust to pay off the gambling debt.

Brody waved his hands. "Wait. Whoa. Don confessed? When?"

"Earlier this afternoon."

"Excuse me?" He cocked a brow.

"Oh, that's right. You don't know." She turned to Marla, who nodded. Lowering her voice, she added, "Don has been talking to me from...well, the afterlife, I guess. He was a ghost."

"Uh-huh, right. Tell me more."

Molly waved her hands. "Well, he's gone now, so there is not much to talk about, except for his confession."

"And that's important, I gather," Marla added.

"Yes."

The conversation lulled while the server came with their food. After a moment of shuffling napkins and flatware, it started again.

"There's more money," she told them.

Both Marla and Brody put down their forks.

"What do you mean?"

"We need to go to the junkyard."

"Why?"

Wiping her mouth from the sticky BBQ, Molly continued. "Well, Don said, right before he left, that there was money in the Grave Dodger. I wonder if it's the fifty-thousand Tattoo Man wanted, which is also why he wanted the truck. I have no clue, just speculating. Since the Grave Dodger is at the junkyard, we need to go there and find the money. Maybe he hid it in a tire, or something. Then we need to pay off Tom Purdy."

Marla shook her head. "Why pay off Tom? I don't understand."

"Because apparently Don embezzled from Two Dudes. He said if I pay off that debt, all is good."

Marla slapped the picnic table. "Let me get this straight. Don said he embezzled money and that you should pay Tom back for what he owed, then all is good. Is that right?"

Molly blinked, thinking back to the conversation. "To be clear, I paraphrased. Don's speech was getting a little sketchy at that point. His words were more like: *Embezzlement. Find Tom. Pay him.*"

"Hmm." Brody rubbed his chin.

"So you think if you just pay off Tom, all is right with the world then, Molly?"

"I think so."

But Brody sat and stared, shaking his head. "No."

Molly was puzzled. "What do you mean?"

"We still don't know if Don's wreck was an accident or intentional."

"True." Molly stared off. "But.... Once, Don said something about Tom being with him in the truck before he died—but according to all the reports, that wasn't the case."

"And Tom is missing," Marla blurted out.

"Perhaps Don was a bit confused, being dead and all," Brody added.

"I don't know." Molly stared at her BBQ sandwich and fries. "Maybe we focus on one thing at a time."

Brody pushed his plate aside. "Let's take a pause. I'd like to sum up what we know or don't know so far." He looked directly at Molly. "Mind if I take a stab at it?"

She shook her head. "Be my guest."

"All right. Sounds like your attorney is off the suspect list. Is that a correct assumption?"

Molly nodded. "I really don't think he's involved at all. I have absolutely nothing to go on with him. While direct, he was also sympathetic and cautioned me about others. I think we can take him off the list."

"Great," Brody said. "Now, what about Tattoo Man."

"I know nothing. He's not appeared for weeks, not since a few days after the funeral."

"Wait," Marla interrupted. "What about the person in the car who shot at the porch flowerpot? Might that have been Tattoo Man?"

Molly shrugged. "No way to know, I guess."

"Hmm." Marla's cell phone binged. She glanced at it, and frowned.

"Who is it?"

Marla's gaze rose. "Mitzi. She wants to know where we are because she's almost home. She and Ken had a fight."

"Oh, shit."

Marla texted Mitzi back.

Brody angled toward Molly again. "Switching subjects—so what about this Hank Carola guy and the Louisiana Republic issue? Is that all resolved?"

Nodding, Molly said, "Yes. Hank was Don's uncle, now deceased. Don found out he'd withheld the trust money for years, but he came clean before he died. All the trust funds are in my name now, for me and the kids."

"Okay. Crossing Hank off the list. That leaves Tom."

Marla looked up from her phone. "Who is AWOL."

All three exchanged glances, then Marla said, "I think we need to go back to the construction office and see what we can find there."

"Maybe." Molly signaled for the check. "But first, I want to go somewhere else. Do you two have time to go to the junkyard with me tonight to look for that money?"

Brody interjected. "Molly, I hate to tell you this, but that truck would not have gone to the junkyard. It's probably worth two hundred grand, no matter its condition. I'm betting it wasn't destroyed in the accident. Besides, it's the Grave Dodger. That truck is famous just for its name and its history."

"But someone told me it went to the junkyard."

"Who?" Marla asked.

Molly's brain swam, trying to remember back to the night of the accident. "I'm not sure. That night, there were so many people at the scene. I remember a wrecker and the state police. All I know is I asked about where they were taking the truck and that's what they said."

"Maybe they were talking about the truck Don was driving?"

"Maybe. But something feels off about all of this...."

"It does." Marla agreed.

"I'm with the two of you," Brody added.

Silence fell over their table for a few minutes as all three pondered. After a minute, Molly snapped her fingers. "Maybe there isn't money hidden in the truck."

"But Don said..."

Molly shook her head. "Don said 'there is money in the truck' but that doesn't necessarily mean hard cash. Like Brody said, that truck is worth a lot of money."

"Well, shit," Marla said. "Is someone breaking it down for parts and selling it off piece by piece?"

"But who?"

"Hells bells," Molly said. "If that is the case, I'm sure now why Don was so restless. That truck was his baby and to have it dismantled so...."

"And now that he's set you on a path to find the truck, he can rest easy."

"You may be right," Molly said. "But then again, where in the hell *is* the Grave Dodger?"

Brody cleared his throat. "Leave that to me. I know a few chop shops in the area, but we are not going there tonight."

"You turn into a pumpkin at midnight?" Marla snickered.

He grinned. "No. Those boys are not to be reckoned with. I'd rather approach them in the light of day."

Molly glanced at her sister. Marla wasn't often bothered but her expression told a different story now.

Brody continued. "Honestly, I think it's best we all go home, get some rest, think through things, and regroup tomorrow. We've gone over a lot of info tonight and we don't want to miss anything. I have some things to take care of in the morning, but I'll be done by two. Let's meet at Molly's house at three." He scanned the group, stopping to linger on Molly. "Work for you?"

While she was hoping to get something done tonight, she understood Brody's intention. "Sure."

Abruptly, Mitzi rushed into the group and plopped down beside Brody. "Hells bells, you all," she said. "What the heck have I missed? Marla said we're raiding Don's office tonight? Is that true? Count me in because I'm loaded for bear. That husband of mine is an ass!"

Molly rolled her eyes. *Oh, sister....*

"Change of plans." Marla stood and reached for Mitzi's hand. "C'mon, let's go get a beer. I'll explain on the way."

Chapter Eight

The two sisters left, and Molly sat directly across from Brody, twiddling her thumbs, so to speak. He stared at her for a full minute, his gaze raking over her face. She ogled him back, making eye contact and silently daring him to pull away first. Finally, the server came with the check and Molly slapped her hand down on it before Brody could react.

He chuckled. "You're a fast one." The sly, sexy, sideways smile his lips made caused her toes to curl a little in her canvas slip-ons.

Pulling a credit card out of her wallet, she stood. "I guess it's time to go. I'll take care of this up front."

She moseyed toward the cashier without a backward glance. Was he following her? Stupid. She should have said something more before leaving. Like, goodbye and thanks for everything, Brody. Instead, she awkwardly snatched up the bill and strolled away.

Molly frowned as the cashier took her card and the check, swiped the card, then handed her the slip of paper. Adding a healthy tip, Molly totaled and signed, then gave pen and paper back to the cashier, looking up.

The young woman grinned. Then, leaning forward, whispered, "He's a hunk." Her eyebrows waggled.

"What?"

The cashier yanked her head toward the exit. Molly glanced that way. Brody stood by the door, leaning into the doorframe, waiting for her—in all his tall, handsome, sexy, and tattooed glory. Her breath nearly left her. "Oh. Yeah. He is, isn't he?"

She smiled back at the woman, who winked. "Dreamy. Have fun tonight."

Grinning at the thought of what a dreamy night with Brody Willis might be like, she strode past him. Her smile broadened when he caught up with her, and her heart tingled a bit when he put his hand in the small of her back. They walked across the parking lot toward the caddy, stopping beside the driver's side door.

She faced him. "How did you know this was my car?"

"Are you kidding?" He let go of a cackle. "Who else in town owns a lavender Cadillac?"

Molly acknowledged the ridiculousness of her words and laughed too. "Right."

Quickly then, Brody swept her closer, wrapping himself around her. His hard, muscled arms felt good against her bare back—she felt safe, protected. Different from how Don made her feel but...nice. Yes. This was lovely, actually.

With her head tipped up, she rested her cheek against his scruffy neck. His warm embrace was inviting, comforting, calming even.

She sighed.

He smelled good, too. Nice.

Really nice. Like leather and coffee and man musk and maybe a little bourbon.

She could get lost in his scent.

"Drive home safely, Molly," he whispered, hugging her

tighter. His breath felt warm against her ear. "I'll see you tomorrow."

He pulled back and peered into her eyes for a moment, softly ran a forefinger over her chin, then stepped away.

Molly nodded. "Yes. Tomorrow."

Brody gave her that sideways, sexy grin again.

Her toes curled. Again.

She watched him head across the parking lot to his Harley, get on the machine, kick-start it into action, rev up the engine, and peel out of the parking lot.

Sigh. Molly blew out a lengthy breath, hoping to compose the quake in her pelvic region.

Oh, Brody Willis, you wicked man you....

* * *

Hours later, at home and in her bed, she realized she might as well give up.

She couldn't sleep.

That was her best, and only, defense.

The bed was lumpy. The house was too quiet.

She'd relived, at least a thousand times, the scene in the parking lot with Brody squealing away on his Harley. He'd not only revved the motorcycle's engine, he'd jumpstarted something in her sexual engine, too.

Damn him. Timing was everything, and she had yet to determine if the timing was right to add Brody Willis to her life.

After all, Don had only been gone two months and one week now.

Don. Crap.

His words wouldn't let her rest, either.

The money is in the Grave Dodger.

"So, are you out there somewhere, asshole? If so, please

show your face and tell me if we are on the right track. How valuable is that stupid truck of yours, anyway?" She stared up at the ceiling, into the dark, hoping to goad him into coming back and talking with her.

Any conversation—even with a ghost—would be welcome at this point.

But Don didn't respond, and she only felt slightly crazier because of it.

It was time to let Don go.

Still, she had to find the money, and the truck, and the sooner the better. Things had to get back to semi-normal. She needed semi-normal, at least.

Something had to happen tonight. She couldn't lie here and do nothing any longer.

Junkyard? No.

Chop shop? Not without Brody.

Don's office? Ah. Perhaps.

She had every right. Correct?

Molly stripped the bed coverings away from her body and got up. She glanced at the clock on the antique nightstand. The time was two-forty-six in the morning.

No time like the present.

Chapter Nine

Molly's heart raced as the echo of footsteps grew closer to Don's office door. As she had hoped, the back door to his office was still unlocked, so access to the inside was easy enough. Figuring out what she was looking for in the dark with only her flashlight, however, had proved rather fruitless.

Still, she'd been an idiot to come here alone, especially since she'd told no one what she was up to.

Moving further into the kneehole under Don's desk, she tried to calm herself—but panic surged through her veins as the lock on the office door jiggled. Instinctively, she reached for her phone and dialed Marla's number, fearing a text wouldn't wake her.

Marla groggily answered after the third ring. "Uh. Hullo."

"Marla," Molly whispered.

"Huh?"

"*Marla*," she hissed. "I'm in trouble."

"Wha...? Where the hell are you?"

"Don's office. I was looking for something. I may have tripped an alarm, not sure, and the police are here." She paused, listening. "At least I think it's the police. Someone is here, in this building."

"Good God, Molly. Stay calm and hidden if you can. Stall them if you can't. I'm on my way."

"Roger that." Molly nodded into the dark and tucked herself further back under Don's enormous desk. Soon after, her phone binged—way too loudly—and she quickly silenced the ringer. *Shit.*

Text message notifications popped up.

Marla: *Mitzi. Wake up. 9-1-1. Don's office. State.*

Mitzi: *What time is it?*

Marla: *No time to explain. Molly is in trouble.*

Mitzi: *Shit. Coming.*

Molly: *Hey. So far so good. The police, or whoever, are still outside the office.*

Mitzi: *Police?*

Molly: *Maybe.*

Mitzi: *WTF are you doing?*

Molly: *Long story. Explain later. Might need your quick thinking and Mitzi magic to get me out of this one. You know I'm not good at making up stories.*

Marla: *Or alibis. Be there in ten.*

Mitzi: *I'm half out the door.*

Molly: *Good. Thanks. They just unlocked the door. Going dark.*

Immediately after typing that, the office door burst open, and the lights flashed on. Startled, Molly cried out a little, and then scrambled to send another text. *Found me*, was all she had time to send (did she even push send?) before a man's booted feet shuffled in front of the desk, and his body bent to look underneath.

He reached under the desk, grasped her arm, and heaved

her out. "Molly Campbell, get out from under there. What the hell are you doing? I could have shot you."

Molly batted Tom Purdy's hand away and scooted out. Standing her ground and looking him square in the face, she asked, "Did you kill my husband? And where the hell is the Grave Dodger?"

Tom squared himself. "Now, Molly. Calm down. Let me explain."

"And where the fuck have you been for weeks now? I want answers."

Tom grabbed her arm and yanked her toward him. "Come with me. We need to talk."

Molly jerked back and shouted. "Oh, no you don't, Tom. I'm not going anywhere with you. Whatever you have to say to me, you can do it right here." She figured her best defense was to stay put. At least she knew she had two potential exits from this room. If she went anywhere with him, she'd likely lose her upper hand.

Tom crowded up closer, and in the same motion, jerked her toward his chest. He stared down with a cool, icy black stare. "Look. I don't want to hurt you, Molly. I won't hurt you. You've been through enough. Let's just go to my office and I can explain everything."

Molly squirmed away from him. "No."

"It's not like you have a choice here, darling. You get that, right?"

But she would not be intimidated by Don's business partner. Molly stood her ground. "What are you going to do, kill me too?"

Movement caught her eye at the back door. A shadow stepped forward and a flash of something shiny caught her eye. Brody stepped into the light. "Let her go, Purdy. Put your hands where I can see them."

"Brody?" Molly murmured.

She vaulted out of Tom's grasp.

Tom stepped back, looked directly at Brody, and raised his hands. "I'm unarmed, man."

Brody stealthily moved forward, glaring at Tom, his Glock pointed at his chest. He nodded to Molly. "Check his pockets, his waistband."

"Got it." Molly quickly approached Tom, patted down his pockets front and back, and his calves. "Kick your boots off, Tom," she ordered.

"What the heck, Molly."

"Do it, man." Brody took a step closer with the Glock, now inches from Tom's face.

"I told you I'm unarmed."

"The boots." Molly poked his arm. "Keep your hands up but kick them off."

Tom reluctantly toed one heel, then the other, kicking off the boots. A small Derringer slid across the floor when one boot came off. Molly kicked it out of Tom's reach.

"I figured that," Molly said. She lifted both of Tom's pant legs and discovered a knife strapped to one ankle. "Neither you or Don went anywhere without a knife and a handgun tucked somewhere."

"Good work, Molly." Brody tugged her to his side, but kept his gaze pinned on Tom. "The gig is up, Purdy. Don't move a muscle."

As if on cue, Marla and Mitzi stumbled through the back door.

* * *

"Well, well. All the Newberry sisters in one place. How charming." Tom Purdy stared at Brody.

"What's going on here?" Mitzi screeched.

Marla nudged her sister and frowned.

"Hush," Molly said. She didn't take her eyes off Tom. "I need answers. I hope you are ready to give them."

Tom sneered. "Seems to me you're the one breaking the law here. Care to explain?"

"This is my husband's office and I'm half-owner now, Tom. I have every right to be here." She glared back.

He laughed. "Right. No. That's not true."

"It is."

"Says who?"

She took a step toward him. Brody placed his hand on her arm, and she halted. "My attorney. And you know it too, because according to Jackson, you want to buy me out. Correct?"

Tom hesitated. "I..."

Brody repositioned his gun, still pointing directly at Tom. "Look, Mr. Purdy. We need to know some things, so let's just cut the crap and get to the facts. How were you involved in Don Campbell's death?"

Tom glowered at Brody for a lengthy spell, then spit out, "If you think I'm going to give you some sort of confession, or explanation for how Don died, then think again. It was an accident, plain and simple. I saw it all happen from the truck behind."

Molly, who had been watching the intense expression on Brody's face, whipped her head around to gawk at Tom. "Wait. What? Weren't you in the truck with Don at the time of the accident?"

Don shook his head. "Before, not during. We argued for the first hour of the trip, so when we stopped for gas, I got out and told him I was riding with Benny Jenkins, who was following us."

"Benny? Don's mechanic?"

"Yes. He generally went to shows in case something went wrong with the Dodger."

"So you didn't kill him."

"No. Why would I kill him? I needed Don to help me get out of the mess I'd put myself in over the past few months. That's why I had to disappear."

Marla stepped forward. "Ah, the plot thickens. Go on."

"I had to lie low for a while. Some threats were made on my life."

Molly pondered that. "Because it was you who was in trouble with the casino, and not Don?"

Tom held her gaze. "Mostly. Some of the trouble we got into together—you know, boys will be boys and we've had a lifetime of it—but most of it was my fault. Especially when I started stealing from the company."

Molly's head started spinning. "*You* embezzled from Two Dudes?" Had she heard Don wrong, the last thing he'd said? "But I thought Don was the one stealing money from the company. What am I missing?"

Tom waved his hands. "Let's back up here a minute."

But Molly was on a roll. "Uh-uh. If you didn't kill Don, then who did?"

"Molly." Tom's voice lowered. "No one intentionally killed Don. I saw it all from behind. A big dog ran across the highway and Don swerved to miss it. It caused the trailer with the Dodger to shift and jack-knife, then Don crossed two lanes of traffic and ended up on the wrong side of the highway, right in the path of a fully loaded tractor-trailer rig. He was gone in an instant."

Molly blinked, still staring at him. "So he was not murdered."

"No."

She narrowed her gaze. "How do I know you are telling me the truth, Tom?"

He glared back. "I suppose you don't. But if we can go into my office, I can prove some other things."

Molly exchanged a glance with Brody.

He nodded. "All right. Lead the way, Purdy. I'm right behind you with my Glock pointed at your back. Move it."

Tom led the way out of the room and across the hall, where he unlocked his office. Molly, Brody, and the sisters followed. When he got to his desk, Tom turned around and looked directly at her. "There's a ledger in the upper right-hand desk drawer with bank information. I can explain everything. What do you want to know?"

Molly ticked her head at Marla, who rushed over to the desk, opened the door, and pulled out a ledger. She leafed through it and nodded. "Lots here to go through."

"Great," Molly said. "I want to know how much money Don owed you. And I want to know if you are responsible for the guy shooting up my Gran's flowerpot, and why Tattoo Man demanded fifty thousand dollars and the truck and to exhume Don's body. I want to know it all, Tom Purdy, including where you've been for the past two months. Got it? So start talking, buster."

Tom glanced around the room. "Well, I might as well come clean. Molly, you've got witnesses here so whatever you decide to do with this information is up to you, I guess. I was the one taking money from the accounts. I transferred it into another bank account and paid off my gambling debts. I was in deep, and Don was trying to help me out because he feared we were going to lose the business. It was tanking fast."

"How was he helping?"

"He had a trust fund—you know the one? He took that money and paid off my debts."

Molly studied him. "I thought he paid off *his* debts and our second mortgage. My house was under foreclosure because Don squandered away our cash."

Tom shook his head. "Not true. Oh, he gambled some and had some debt, but mine was monstrous and he did what he could to help. Maxine had left me by then, and I hadn't seen the kids in months. I was depressed and frankly, not in a good place. Don wanted to help."

Brody lowered his gun and cleared his throat. "So let me get this straight. You were the gambler, and the majority of the debt was yours—but Don took money out of his trust to pay off your debt, his small debt, and the second mortgage on his house. Why would he do that?"

Tom nodded. "Like he said, he feared losing the business. I'd taken thousands of dollars from the account. I oversaw finances, so Don rarely looked at the books. Besides embezzling money, I also defaulted on several loans, and we lost a couple of large contracts because of it. Two Dudes was going under." He turned to Molly. "He took out the second mortgage on your house when he found out how much I owed and that I was skimming funds from the business accounts to pay the casino collectors. When he pulled money from that trust, your second mortgage was paid off first."

Molly angled her head, thinking. "But I got foreclosure notices and calls from the bank."

He nodded. "They were fake. I made the calls and sent the notices. There's a folder in my desk with copies."

Molly nodded to Mitzi, who started going through other desk drawers.

"But why?"

"I know," Mitzi interjected. "After Don died, your cash cow was gone, so you were going to force Molly to sell out of everything—her house, the business—and blackmail her for the cash."

"In a way," Tom confessed. "I wanted to scare you into selling, Molly. I sent the guy who shot the flowerpot at your Gran's, but I have no idea who this Tattoo Man is you are talking about."

Molly swallowed. Hard. So someone else was involved? Who had she missed?

Brody stepped closer to Tom. "Where is the Grave Dodger? What happened to it after the wreck?"

"That's right," Molly said. "Where is it?"

Tom's face went blank. "I haven't a clue. I wish I knew."

Behind her, high heels clicked on the tile floor, and the sound of a gun cocking behind her head grabbed her attention. Molly froze.

"Fortunately, or unfortunately, as it may be for you, I know the answers to both questions."

Molly heard the woman's words and simultaneously felt the cold snub of a pistol nudge her neck, right behind her ear. She watched her sisters' eyes grow wide. Brody scowled and raised his gun again, pointing it at her assailant.

Mitzi gasped, clapping a hand over her mouth.

"Jillie Dilly," Marla hissed. "What the fuck?"

"In the flesh, bitches."

Molly resisted the urge to turn around and punch the woman in the face. That's when Brody lowered his gun and shot Jillie Dilly in the foot.

* * *

An uncanny silence ranged over the small room. Then, Jillie screamed, tossing her gun aside. "You shot my toes! You idiot. My new Jimmy Choos! My fucking pedicure!"

The door banged open again and two of Carrington's finest law enforcement officers burst inside, guns poised.

"Well, what do we have here? Breaking and entering, I presume?" The first officer quipped, kicking Jillie's gun aside. He strode on into the room, assessing the situation. A younger officer tailed him.

"Breaking and entering? Officer, you give us far too much credit." Marla interjected with some quick wit. "We were merely taking an extended tour of Don's office, courtesy of a misplaced key."

Mitzi added to the banter. She stared at the officer's name badge. "Officer Jones, we thought we'd play a little game of '*Clue: The Intruders Edition.*' You seem to have figured it out."

"Are you mocking me?"

Marla continued. "Oh, no, officer. I wouldn't dare. Just appreciating the fine art of law enforcement."

Officer Jones took one look at Brody, gun still in his hand, and said to the other officer, "Cuff him."

Molly's nerves tightened. "No! Cuff her." She pointed to Jillie. "That's her gun on the floor. Brody was only protecting us."

"That so. Huh." The officer frowned.

Molly figured she had to get a handle on this situation. "Look, officers, it's not what it seems. This is my deceased husband's office—my office now—and we were just trying to find some things when this gentleman..." She swept her hand toward Tom. "My ex-business partner, interrupted us."

Mitzi stepped forward. "Actually, he just confessed to embezzlement, so he's your guy. Cuff him."

Officer Jones smirked. "Give me a break here, ladies."

Molly gave her full attention to the officers. "We're telling the truth. No breaking or entering here. This man, and the woman with the bleeding toes, are the problems. Not us."

The second officer wasn't buying it. "Save it, lady. We've heard it all before. You're going downtown.

Marla smirked. "Oh, officer, downtown is so yesterday. Dank and dirty, or so we've heard. Don't you have something with a view?"

"Yeah. Maybe something in blue to match our eyes."

"You are making fun of us."

Brody stepped forward. "Gentlemen, please. These ladies might be a tad overzealous in their amateur detective work, but their hearts are in the right place. How about we let them off with a friendly warning?"

Molly stepped between them. "No. How about you cuff the dame and the dude there, and cart them off to jail? I'm filing charges of embezzlement and misuse of company funds and assets. Maybe attempted kidnapping and murder. I can go down to the station right now and take care of that."

Officer Jones cocked a brow. "You have proof?"

Marla raised the ledger. "Right here. Embezzlement. And I'll just add, from what I can tell here, that Miss Jillian Dillon over there, had her hand in the embezzlement pie too. In fact, if I were a betting woman—which I am not because we know that gets people into trouble, right Mr. Purdy?—I'd also venture a guess to say that Tom Purdy and Jillie Dillon were having an affair."

Mitzi gasped. "How?"

"Because quite a few checks were written to one Jillian Dillon. Not to mention several written for cash, which will be difficult to trace, but that is the point. Isn't it?"

Molly eyeballed Tom, then Jillie. "Is that true?"

"Well, let me explain..." said Tom.

Molly stomped her feet and clenched her fists. "No! I've had enough of your explaining! Out of my business. Get them out. I'm filing charges."

Officer Jones gave her a begrudging nod. He and his fellow

officer cuffed both Tom and Jillie, reciting their rights as they led them out the door.

Molly heaved a sigh. "Well, that was fun."

"That was ridiculous," Marla exclaimed. "I can't believe that just happened."

"Are we amateur detectives now, Brody? Can we go into business with you?"

Brody arched a brow. "No. And the next time, leave the investigating to the professionals." He grinned at Molly.

She felt a mischievous grin spread across her face. "Thank you, Brody," she directed to him. "I've learned my lesson. Next time I'll stay away from the crime scene and leave the genuine detective work to you."

"Nothing like a woman who knows her place." Brody reached for her and pulled her closer. "And I like your place being right here," he whispered.

Molly looked up into his eyes and grew slightly dizzy. "It's a fine place," she murmured.

"Um. Okay, you two. Get a room, please?" Mitzi circled the desk.

Marla picked up the ledger and stuffed it under her arm. "Let's get down to the station so you can file that paperwork, Molly. I'm hungry. Anyone else want to get something to eat?"

"Me!" Mitzi joined her.

"The only thing open at this hour is the Waffle Shack," Molly said.

Brody grinned. "I'm up for waffles."

"Ditto."

"Me, too."

"Beat you there."

Chapter Ten

Molly stepped back and let Brody handle the Channellock, snapping the deadbolt off the door to the large metal building on Halifax Street, down the road several blocks from the Two Dudes Construction office.

"Well ladies, now or never, I guess," he said, reaching to hoist up the oversized garage door. "Let's hope Tom and Jillie were telling the truth."

"Wait." Molly put a hand over Brody's. "Give me a second."

Marla felt her sister's forehead. "Are you feeling okay?"

Molly nodded. "Yes. It's just that last night, and this morning, and really this whole damn week has been such a whirlwind. I want to savor this moment for just a bit—if the Grave Dodger is in there, then I think all the pieces have fallen together. Right? Nothing will be left unturned?"

Mitzi stepped forward and gave Molly a hug. "I think you're right. I swear, I didn't know Jillie Dilly had it in her to be so scheme-y."

"I know!" Molly bounced her gaze from both her sisters to Brody. "Tom said she was the brains of the embezzlement plan."

"She even pulled her brother in on the scheme too. Can you believe he is Tattoo Man?"

Marla nodded. "I think he was in my class in elementary school. Was such a weenie back then. Interesting."

"Can you believe she even confessed to cutting Don's brake lines enough so he would gradually lose brake fluid, and then potentially not be able to stop on the interstate?"

"So the dog story was fake, too." Mitzi shook her head.

"I can't believe she actually confessed to that," Marla said.

"I know. I feel a little sorry for Tom." Molly shrugged, looking at Brody.

"Well, I don't," he said. "Tom was in just as deep as Jillie."

"He was desperate. I guess he hung on to anything Jillie suggested just to keep afloat."

"Well, all I know," Marla said, staring at the garage, "is that if the Grave Dodger isn't in here, we still have some detective work to do."

Mitzi grinned and nudged Molly. "Hey Brody, maybe you could take us on as part-timers." She grinned.

He quickly shook his head. "I'm a one-man show, Mitzi. Sorry." Then immediately, his gaze met Molly's and he grinned that sexy, sideways smile that never failed to curl her toes. She grinned back.

"Let's get this over with," she said. "Brody?"

"All right." He grasped the handle again and tugged upward.

Sunlight beamed into the door from behind them, glinting off the shiny chrome of one monstrous Ford pickup truck.

Marla sighed. "She is pretty, isn't she?"

"I always loved that ghostly vision painted on the side," Mitzi added.

"She's still on the trailer. That's convenient."

"Yes. And none too worse for the wear." Molly stepped

inside the garage, looking over the monster motor vehicle. "Banged up a little but surprisingly not too bad."

Marla studied the truck. "I can't believe that Don's truck was smashed into oblivion but this one survived."

"I bet the hitch was knocked loose. Maybe." Brody shrugged. "Can't say for certain. I'm a bike guy not a truck guy."

Molly turned and faced Brody. "What do you think, though. Still in pretty good shape?"

"Yep. Are you going to keep it or sell it?"

Looking back at the truck, she shook her head. "I'm not sure. Might keep it for the kids. To remember their dad by."

Brody took her hand. "That's a great idea."

"I guess I should call a tow truck to pull her back to my old house—which by the way, goes off the market later today. I called the agent."

"You do have that big three-car garage there."

"Yes. That's where Don always kept her."

The four of them stared at the truck for a moment, then Marla said, "Well, I hate to break up a party, but I have to run. I need some sleep before tonight. There is a Grateful Dead cover band playing at Cooter's tonight up in Shreveport."

"Can I come too? Ken is still in Texas and I'm still mad at him."

Marla grinned. "Of course. Let's go get some sleep." They waved their goodbyes and left.

Molly sighed. "I want to check something—just out of curiosity." She went to the driver's side of the truck, climbed up on the trailer, and stretched to open the door. She looked back at Brody as she fumbled around on the floorboard. "Don always kept his pistol stashed under here when he was driving. Maybe I should get it."

Grasping the leather gun case, she tugged it out from under the seat. "I thought so."

Brody helped her down from the trailer.

Molly unzipped the case. Several hundred-dollar bills fluttered to the ground—and there were more stashed inside the leather bag.

She might never truly know the depth of Don's deception—was he telling the truth about his involvement with Tom? But at the very least, he always took good care of them.

Molly looked down at the money and grinned. *Thanks, Don.*

* * *

The End! Thanks for reading *Seriously Dead*! I hope you enjoyed this story, and also that you've read *Freshly Dead*, Book 1, too. I'd love it if you'd leave a review wherever you purchased this book, or at my website, www.maddiejamesbooks.com

* * *

Ready for **_Gratefully Dead_, Book 3? Get it today!
Scroll on for a sneak peek!**

Chapter One—Gratefully Dead

Marla Newberry glanced up from her coffee and stared at the yellowed plastic clock on the diner wall. The place smelled of bacon grease, coffee, and the lingering aftermath of someone's flowery perfume. The counter was empty at this hour, most folks having cleared out after the Saturday morning breakfast rush.

The old clock ticked steadily, its hands sweeping the face in unbroken movement.

Tick. Tick. Tick.

Her sisters sat huddled in a corner booth a few feet away, speaking in hushed tones. She'd avoided them ever since they had arrived. Sighing, she ran a hand through her hair and sat up straighter. They were talking about her.

"Give it up, ladies," she called out.

Mitzi smirked. "What?"

"You know."

Molly twisted in her seat. "You gonna mope all day or join us?" Her bright blue eyes flashed with the challenge of her words. Molly was the youngest of the three sisters and never at a loss for words.

Chapter One—Gratefully Dead

Marla stood, smoothing the wrinkles from her faded jeans. "I'm not moping." She lifted her cup and saucer. She loved that the diner used old-fashioned cups and saucers rather than mugs.

"You've been staring into your coffee for an hour," Mitzi added. "Surprised you even saw us come in. Get over here. We were just talking about the Halloween festival next month. Help us plan."

Ah yes, the annual small town, Carrington, Louisiana Halloween Festival. Her family had volunteered for years, and this year would be no different. Marla slid into the booth beside Mitzi, her middle sister.

Mitzi's eyes showed concern, and Marla felt a pang of guilt. Her sisters worried too much.

"Plenty of time for festival planning, you know. I'm sure Mom's on it."

"She is, of course," Molly said. "Dad's doing the dunking booth again."

Of course. Dad loved that thing.

"It is September, you know. October is just around the corner," Mitzi added.

"I know that. School just started." She definitely knew school had started because she was teaching English this year, and her middle schoolers were already kicking her butt.

"Three weeks ago." Molly sipped her coffee. "Ewe. This is cold." She signaled the server behind the counter.

Mitzi widened her eyes, looking directly at Marla. "Distracted much?" She waited for a response, sipping from the straw in her chocolate shake, her cheeks sucking in. "You were lost in thought over there."

"I'm fine. Just lesson planning in my head. I have a job, you know."

Molly snorted. "Nice try. We know you've been thinking about Cooter."

Chapter One—Gratefully Dead

The server came and refilled their coffee cups. Heat rose in Marla's cheeks at the mention of his name. When the young woman left, she said, "I don't know what you mean."

"Oh please," Mitzi scoffed. "You've been wandering around with that confused and pained look on your face for a couple of months now. Ever since you two—"

"Can we talk about something else?" Marla interrupted sharply. She didn't want to think or talk about Cooter Haines or the memory of his lips on hers, warm and tasting of whiskey.

Molly and Mitzi exchanged a glance, then Mitzi squeezed Marla's hand. "Of course. Whatever you want."

The old clock continued its steady beat.

Tick. Tick. Tick.

The sound was barely audible above the din of the traffic outside and voices in the diner, and most people probably didn't even hear it. But she did. Why was she so focused on it?

Was time running out? For what?

Her heart, however, beat anything but steady. She stared into her coffee again, wishing for the familiar comfort of routine. But since the random and impromptu and decadent and subsequently repetitive encounters with Cooter started a few months ago, nothing was routine anymore.

It wasn't like her to be so enamored of a man that he occupied her every living and breathing moment, every thought in her brain. She was more of a love 'em and leave 'em kind of girl. Er, woman. She and Cooter had shared a warm and friendly relationship for a couple of years—it had always been hands and lips off—until it wasn't.

Until about six months ago.

Tick. Tick. Tick.

At first it had been delicious fun—scrambling off to the storeroom in the back or sneaking up to his apartment over the bar. Neither of them had talked about anything more than an

Chapter One—Gratefully Dead

occasional toe-touching romp—easing the tension of the week and having a little whisky-induced fun.

Until the last time, a couple of months ago, and Cooter had gotten serious.

So serious, in fact, he'd mentioned the L-word.

Marla wasn't ready for the L-word. She made that quite clear that night.

She'd not seen him since.

It wasn't him.

It was her.

Tick. Tick. Tick.

Mitzi patted the table in front of Marla. "Earth to sister. Earth to sister. Goodness, that man has you all swoony and everything."

Shaking herself, Marla stuck out her tongue. "Does not." She glanced once more at the clock on the wall, then refused to think about it. Time with Cooter? Running out? Ridiculous.

"Whatever. Hey. I was thinking of going out tonight. Hubby is in New Orleans on business. Want to go to Shreveport?"

Molly grinned. "I do. Brody is off work tonight. I could see him."

"Good. He hangs out at Deadhead, right?" Mitzi then focused on Marla. "You're coming too. No excuse."

Deadhead was Cooter's bar. Marla shook her head. "No. I've... I have other plans."

Mitzi dismissed that. "I think Skull Bone is playing there tonight. Do you know for sure?"

What the heck was she getting at? Cooter was the drummer for Skull Bone, a Grateful Dead tribute band. He was super awesome with the sticks, one of the best drummers around. They played Deadhead often, so it wasn't really a big deal. Shrugging, she said, "More than likely."

"Then go with us."

Chapter One—Gratefully Dead

She shook her head. "No. Plans, remember?"

Tick. Tick. Tick.

Damn it. Stop.

Molly gestured with a hand. "Oh, pooh. Change them."

She shouldn't. But she kind of wanted to. "I don't know. I have to think about it. Call you later?"

Mitzi stood, grabbing the check. "Just make sure you do, sister. Don't give us the slip. We'll be there by nine."

Marla nodded. "Fine."

Looking proud and pleased, Mitzi's grin widened. "I'm picking up your coffee, too. See you later."

Marla watched them leave. They'd done it to her again.

* * *

Late in the afternoon, Marla went for a hike at Kisatchie National Forest to clear her head, and to keep her from thinking about Cooter and going to Shreveport and the biker bar. She'd willed herself to stop thinking about ticking clocks and time running out. That was all weird, anyway—that old clock.

Instead, she simply wanted to clear her brain and get some exercise to tire out her body.

She could have ridden her bike, her Harley—it was a beautiful afternoon for it—but decided instead to take the jeep. The hike would exhaust her. She didn't need to ride home on the bike.

Exhaustion was perhaps what she needed right now. She'd not slept well lately and could use a good night's sleep.

The worn trail stretched before her as she made her way into the woods, sunlight filtering through the canopy above. The sun streamed through the trees, creating a shifting, shimmering layer of light and shadow. Her boots crunched on the pine

Chapter One—Gratefully Dead

needle-strewn path, a soothing rhythm that calmed her soul somewhat.

Outside of a warbling bird and an occasional squirrel's chatter, the forest was quiet—and she felt at peace. She could lose herself in the winding trails and the solitude.

She quickened her pace. The trail sloped upwards, straining her muscles, and she savored the burn in her thighs. It had been a while since she'd had a good physical workout. Fatigue quieted her restless mind, and for a while she thought of nothing but the terrain ahead.

Nothing like a long hike to put things into perspective.

By the time she returned to her Jeep, dusk had crept into daylight. She drove back toward Carrington with the windows down; the air scented with pine and promise. After about an hour of driving and musing, she realized she was at a crossroads.

Literally.

Turn left to go to Carrington and home. Right would take her to Shreveport and The Deadhead.

Impulsively, she turned toward Shreveport.

Damn it. Was this a mistake?

She drove on.

Some nights the stars shone so brightly they lit the country road, but tonight clouds obscured the sky. Marla wondered if that was an omen of doom. What would Cooter think, her showing up again? Now?

An hour later, she pulled into the gravel lot of The Deadhead.

Neon signs glowed in the dimness, advertising Lone Star beer and Jim Beam. From within came the familiar strains of "Friend of the Devil," a frequently played Grateful Dead song at the bar.

Marla gripped the steering wheel, her heart pounding.

The Deadhead biker bar sat near the end of town, in a

Chapter One—Gratefully Dead

secluded area. Cooter had told her once that when he bought the place, and told others he was opening a bar there, that they laughed. It was too far out of town, they said. No one would come all the way out there for a beer.

But Cooter thought otherwise and persevered. They came for the beer, the atmosphere, and the music. And they came often.

The loud music and revved up bikes didn't bother anyone, which was a good thing, because both were loud and often. She hadn't been to Deadhead in weeks, avoiding the surge of longing and desire Cooter's presence evoked. But tonight, the lure of music and memory proved too strong.

Tick. Tick. Tick.

"Oh, stop it. Damn it! I'm going."

Looking down at herself, still dressed in hiking shorts and a T-shirt, desperately needing a shower, and shook her head. Not bar clothes, that was for certain. Not that the patrons of The Deadhead really cared.

Which they didn't.

She got out of the Jeep and walked to the entrance, pushing open the creaking wooden door. The smoky interior was crowded, as always, bikers and locals mingling over pool tables and beers.

Marla sighed, glancing around the dimly lit interior. She loved the atmosphere, the live music and cold beer—she was more than ready for a cold one, to be honest.

She'd long ago decided she preferred the untamed atmosphere of The Deadhead, having grown tired of the safe, quaint, and predictable, small-town scene in Carrington. The men there were fine for happily-ever-after, but she was more of a casual fling woman. No man she'd ever met in Carrington shared her thirst for adventure or understood her free spirit.

And as a teacher, she also couldn't afford any gossip or

drama. Her students would have a field day if they saw her out with a different man every weekend. Middle school kids were the worst. It was simpler to avoid local dating altogether.

She wasn't fond of the music row bar scene near the river in downtown Shreveport, either. A bit on the seedier side of life, she'd braved it when she was younger and with a group of her girlfriends. Bar hopping was a thing back then, right out of college. But now, Cooter's place was where she wanted to be, for the beer, an occasional whiskey sour, and of course, Cooter.

Marla's gaze drifted to the leather-topped bar. A crowd of men and women huddled up against it. She'd met Cooter sitting at that bar two years ago and had bonded instantly over their mutual love of the Grateful Dead and motorcycle road trips.

While Marla cherished her independence, she couldn't deny the connection between them. Cooter was a talented drummer, and she loved the music. He owned a bar, and she liked beer and whiskey. Like Marla, he had a Harley and craved the freedom and new experiences the open road offered.

When she was with Cooter, her heart raced with excitement and possibility.

And there. There he was, standing behind the bar—tall and rugged in worn jeans and a leather vest, pushing his shoulder-length and graying hair away from his face, while drawing beers from the tap, and talking up the customers.

Cooter. Her Cooter?

Marla stood frozen in place, caught between leaving and rushing into his arms. Their last encounter had been bitter and painful, a clash of stubborn wills that left her aching with loss. But one look at Cooter, and she knew nothing had really changed. Her heart belonged to him, much as she hated to admit it. It was beating terribly erratic—as wild and as primitive as the bayou at midnight.

As if sensing her gaze, Cooter looked up and caught her eye.

Chapter One—Gratefully Dead

He checked a slow smile easing across his face. Her insides melted a little.

Marla smiled back, warmth flooding her veins.

She swallowed hard and slid onto a stool near the end. Cooter placed a Lone Star in front of her without a word.

She might avoid most men in Carrington, but she would always come back for Cooter. He was her one exception.

She took a long sip, savoring the sharp, familiar taste. "Skull Bone playing tonight?" She tried to sound casual, nonchalant, and wondered if it was working.

"Nah. Next weekend. Bayou Jam is here." Cooter's voice was a rough rumble.

"Ah." Marla took another drink of beer. "Shoot. I told Molly and Mitzi that Skull Bone was playing. I think they were going to make it up. I should text them." She pulled her phone out of her back pocket.

"You coming around again now?"

His question made her pause, and she slowly set the phone face down on the bar, the text unsent.

"I don't know." Marla traced a pattern in the condensation on her beer bottle, glancing about at the crowd, not making eye contact. "Been a few weeks."

"Eight weeks. Two months. Five days."

She met his gaze then. He knew exactly how long? "Oh."

"You're the one who left." There was an edge to Cooter's words. "Said you needed time away from this place. From me."

"I know." She held his gaze, unmoving. "But I couldn't stay away. Not from the music, and... Not from you."

Cooter stared, his expression unreadable, except for a flicker of longing in his eyes that kicked up a response of mixed messages in her heart and gut—of hope and apprehension.

She wanted him. She didn't want him. She wanted him.

The bar erupted in cheers as Bayou Jam took the stage,

Chapter One—Gratefully Dead

launching into their first song. Marla swayed, closing her eyes and losing herself in the familiar chords and lyrics. When she opened them again, Cooter was watching her, a smile tugging at the corner of his mouth.

"Come on," he said, grabbing her hand. "Let's get out of here."

"You can't leave."

"We need to talk." Cooter glanced to his right. "Luke can handle this crowd." He gave the bartender a nod.

Marla watched Cooter's friend, Luke Strong, nod back, then slid her gaze to Cooter. Her heart nearly burst from her chest at the intense look in his eyes. "Where are we going?"

"Anywhere but here." Cooter's smile widened. "The night is young." His eyebrows waggled.

He grabbed a bottle of Jim Beam and led her out the back. Marla laughed, gripped his hand, and followed Cooter to his bike. He stashed the whiskey in a saddlebag. She climbed on behind him, her arms winding around his waist, fingers locking over his hard, taut, six-pack abdomen. The engine roared to life beneath them as they sped off.

Her chest grew warm against his back—from the inside out.

She was home at last.

* * *

The night air rushed over her skin as they sped down the dark, winding roads outside of town. Marla clung to Cooter, overcome with the thrill of it all, no longer questioning her sanity.

This was right.

They arrived at the old, abandoned barn, its silhouette illuminated by the moonlight. She followed him just inside the wide door, her steps tentative but determined. He spread out a blanket on the dirt floor and opened the bottle of whiskey.

Chapter One—Gratefully Dead

They could still see the sky. Marla noticed the clouds had cleared. Stars glittered the night sky. She relaxed a little more.

"We used to come out here a lot when we were kids." He gestured to the dusty bales of hay stacked against one wall. "My uncle owns the place."

Marla cocked her head. "Ah, hay bales, full moons, and young lovers in the night. Was this your favorite spot?"

He laughed. "No girls. Just my guy friends and me, shooting the shit, drinking some beer. Maybe sneaking a smoke." He gave her a wicked grin.

She smiled, inching closer to him until their knees touched. "I don't believe that for a minute."

He threw back his head and laughed again.

He handed her the bottle of Jim Beam. She took a sip, then handed it back. He took a gulp. The fire of the alcohol burned down her throat and filled her with warmth. Seduced by the setting, perhaps, and the man leaning in closer, Marla kissed him—slowly at first, then deeper—until she was lost in his embrace.

Cooter pulled away slightly and brushed his lips across hers again before lying back on the blanket and folding his hands beneath his head. She admired his strong features, illuminated in the moonlight, as he studied her with deep-set eyes that seemed to search through every layer of her being for answers she wasn't sure she had.

He reached for her hand, turning it over so he could trace circles around her palm with his thumb. "Tell me everything," he whispered. "Tell me the problem between us."

Marla let go of her doubts as she spoke. Her voice quavered at first, but grew stronger with emotion.

"Between us?"

He nodded. "How about you talk about how you feel about us? Period."

Marla blew out a breath. "I was feeling like what I knew about myself wasn't true anymore."

He grinned. "I get that."

"I never intended to fall for someone so completely. I don't do relationships, Cooter. I've never been good with them and, frankly, I never wanted one."

His right eyebrow spiked. "Oh? And now?"

She sighed. "I've missed you these past two months. I didn't know what we had was real until I was away from you. All I could think about was getting back to how things were before the night of the argument." She held her breath. "Do you feel the same way?"

Cooter remained silent but gripped her hand throughout her confession until finally nodding in response when she finished speaking.

"Marla, darlin', I can't get enough of you. I need you in my life." It was a simple, heartfelt statement. Just like him. Straightforward and uncomplicated.

Marla tilted her head back with a sigh and gazed up at the stars. "Oh, Cooter...."

"You're beautiful." Cooter propped himself up on an elbow.

She looked at him. "It's just the moonlight."

He touched her cheek with a forefinger, let it linger and then slowly trace the side of her face. "No, it's you."

"It's the stars." Her brain raced, trying to recall if anyone had ever called her beautiful before. Pretty, maybe, but beautiful? "The stars are beautiful."

"Not as beautiful as you." Cooter brushed a stray curl behind her ear. "I'm glad you came to Deadhead that night two years ago. You turned my universe upside down, Marla Newberry."

She looked at him, this easygoing, caring man who had

Chapter One—Gratefully Dead

stormed into her life. "You did the same for me. I never knew I could feel this way about someone."

"Tell me how you feel?" His voice was rough with emotion.

"Like I can be fully myself with you. Like we're two parts of the same whole." She took his hand, threading their fingers together. "You're it for me, Cooter. However long we have in this life, I'm yours. If there's anything after this, I'm yours then, too."

He stared into her eyes for a long moment, as if he were measuring what to say next. Then she guessed he figured he should put it out there again.

"I love you, Marla."

She eased out a sigh and her chest felt lighter. "Cooter," she whispered, "I love you, too." She'd never said those words to another man.

Cooter pulled her in for a searing kiss. Marla gave herself over to the sensation, to him, heart, body, and soul. The next few hours sealed their love with a toe-tingling romp under the stars that Marla knew she would never forget.

They shared a bond as endless as the road ahead and as constant as the stars above. With bone-deep certainty, what they had would endure all tests of time.

Perhaps eternity.

* * *

Get your copy of *Gratefully Dead* today!

Do you get Maddie's Insider News?

Be the first to get the latest news about my books—new releases, free ebooks, sales and discounts, sneak peeks, and exclusive content! Just add your email address at this link: https://maddiejamesbooks.com/pages/newsletter

Whether writing flirty contemporary romance or gritty romantic suspense, Maddie James writes to silence the people in her head.

In 2022, Maddie celebrated her 25th year of publishing romance fiction under multiple pen names. Her collective body of work includes over 70 titles. Maddie loves writing small town contemporary romance and cowboy worlds, and as M.L. Jameson she pens romantic suspense.

Affair de Coeur says Maddie, "shows a special talent for traditional romance," and RT Book Reviews claimed, "James deftly combines romance and suspense, so hope on for an exhilarating ride."

Learn more and buy books direct at www.maddiejamesbooks.com.

Milton Keynes UK
Ingram Content Group UK Ltd.
UKHW010858040923
428018UK00004B/348